She vowed she would never admit he was right

"You are quite the most interfering man I have ever met," Davida protested to Lyall after Hugh said goodbye. "You had no right to send Hugh away."

"No doubt, but any fool could see you wished he would go. Whatever happened to his offer for you? Today I saw him exchanging tender glances with Miss Baugh. Did she cut you out?"

"Of course not," snapped Davida, stung by his bare-bones description of a complicated situation. "I have just declined Hugh's offer, for private reasons."

Lyall looked skeptical. "Never mind," he consoled. "I'm sure a woman of your charms will soon find another soul mate. Perhaps I can help."

"You would do better to find a soul mate of your own," she told him.

"Ah, but I have found one," Lyall returned with a wicked grin, "haven't I?"

CONTRARY LOVERS

CLARICE PETERS

Harlequin Books

TORONTO • NEW YORK • LONDON
AMSTERDAM • PARIS • SYDNEY • HAMBURG
STOCKHOLM • ATHENS • TOKYO • MILAN

For the real Jeremy in my life

Published April 1988
ISBN 0-373-31020-X

CHAPTER ONE

FIVE MINUTES after receiving word that his father was belowstairs in the Blue Saloon urgently requesting speech with
his only son, Lord Lyall quitted his dressing room. He had
been in the midst of his morning toilette when the news of
the Earl of Exley's arrival reached him, but not even the
highest stickler of the ton could fault his appearance now.

Lyall looked exactly what he was acknowledged to be: a
top-of-the-trees Corinthian, impeccably dressed in the palest of buff pantaloons, matching waistcoat, white cravat
starched and arranged in the Trône d'Amour, and a coat of
Bath-blue superfine, which hugged a set of shoulders that
inevitably aroused envy in the breasts of less-endowed
gentlemen. No need for Wilkes, the genius who had custody of his lordship's wardrobe, to invest in moulded
shoulders the way the valets of some of his more unfortunate contemporaries did!

Without apparent haste but with less than his customary
languor, Lyall moved down the Adam staircase, an expression of bemused interest on his face. This visage, while not
classically handsome, was nonetheless appealing, boasting
as it did an aquiline nose, dark, riveting eyes and a pair of
craggy brows which the more impressionable females were
wont to liken to the brooding features of Lord Byron himself.

At the moment, Lyall's mind was troubled not by poetry
but by the Earl of Exley's unexpected appearance under his
roof on this June morning of 1816. At five and fifty his fa-

ther rarely intervened in the lives of his offspring, and the excellence of this tradition was proved in the cordial relationship he enjoyed with both his son and married daughter.

But clearly something must have happened to rouse the earl, a notoriously late riser if memory served correctly, from his comfortable establishment on St. James's Square at the ungodly hour of ten-thirty.

Had the Countess of Exley been alive Lyall might have sensed a domestic squabble afoot, but this avenue was closed to him by his mother's death some twenty years ago, and he was wholly at a loss to determine why his father was visiting.

His musings came to a sudden halt as he neared the Blue Saloon and caught sight of the earl's stout figure pacing from one end of the large room to the other. Strange doings indeed for a man whose ruddy face usually held nothing more alarming than a gleam of satisfaction as he bested his cronies over a hand of whist at Brook's. Clearly, something was amiss.

"Good morning, Papa," Lyall said now, greeting his parent warmly. "This is a great surprise."

"It may be an even greater surprise before the hour is up," the earl prophesied gloomily, turning and dropping into the nearest armchair, which fortunately—since he weighed a good twenty stone at least—was a sturdy Hepplewhite. Lyall was startled by this show of emotion in one whose equanimity was famed throughout London, and he felt at a momentary loss for words. However, Stewart, his butler, was made of sterner stuff, and he held out a tray of restoratives to the earl who, smelling the presence of Madeira nearby, reached out with an impatient hand for some.

Reassured by this familiar sign of life in his sire, Lyall took a glass as well and waited for the earl to begin. But now that the earl was face-to-face with him the reasons behind the morning call had apparently vanished.

Ten minutes passed as the earl belaboured the shortness of bone in one of the bays he had been persuaded to purchase at Tattersall's, and another ten in lavish praise of the Madeira—the earl fancying himself an excellent judge of both horseflesh and wine. At last Lyall, who had been an attentive audience to these particulars, felt obliged to get to the bottom of his father's call.

"You mentioned a surprise, I believe, sir?" he prompted.

The look of gloom which had been chased away by the Madeira descended again on the earl's brow.

"It wasn't my doing, Jeremy," he intoned mournfully, gazing into his glass. "You must know that from the start."

"Indeed, Papa?" Lyall answered, his thoughts swirling about in a fog. "But if you would only be good enough to say just *what* wasn't your doing."

The earl balanced the Madeira on his left knee. "Thought it best to see you myself. I had a chat with Jarvis."

At this mention of his father's solicitor Lyall looked up in surprise.

"Had to call him in," the earl went on, "especially since that chit had the gall to write to me...."

"Chit?" Lyall inquired faintly.

Exley dug deeper into the armchair and nodded. "I suppose you shall have to meet her, Jeremy. She insists upon it."

For a moment Lyall stood with a pinch of Mr. George Berry's finest snuff unnoticed between thumb and forefinger. "Papa," he said, trying not to laugh, "you have not been boxed in by some high flyer, I hope?"

The earl recoiled instantly, his unblemished reputation for propriety rudely scorched. "High flyer!" he expostulated. "Has anyone said a word about the muslin company?"

"No," Lyall acknowledged with a twinkle in his eye. "But you did mention a chit."

"I'm glad you aren't deaf," the earl muttered. "Shouldn't be deaf at your age; three and thirty, ain't it?"

"Two and thirty," came the cheerful reply. "And," Lyall added, "my hearing is alleged to be in perfect condition. Would you mind cutting line and explaining who this chit is?"

"Her name is Miss Cooper."

Lyall, noticing the snuff in his hand, gave it a modest snort, wrinkling up his nose at finding the mixture a shade too dry. As befitted one deemed a matrimonial prize by Lady Jersey herself, he was well acquainted with the names of the reigning beauties. He had never heard of a Miss Cooper, and said so now.

Vexed, the earl put down his glass on the black ormolu table. "Naturally you haven't heard of her. Nor had I until a few days ago. And I heartily wish I hadn't." He waved his son toward the chair opposite him. "For how can a man speak sensibly with you looming over him!"

Lyall, smiling, complied with the request but declared that he did not believe his father was making a pinch of sense at the moment and just what was Miss Cooper to him.

"She's nothing to me!" the earl growled. "Never saw her in my life and that's the plain truth. But," he added grudgingly, "her father was an old acquaintance of mine."

This admission sparked a flurry of speech. "Cutter Cooper, we used to call him. Always a great one for cutting a wheedle." The earl chuckled. "I recollect once when we were both at Oxford together he switched the pepper pot for the salt at the headmaster's table. Notoriously shortsighted chap. The headmaster, I mean, not old Cutter, who got sent down for it of course." He sighed and shook his head. "Pity he's dead now. A year, no, two, or so Miss Cooper says. That's the daughter. There are two of them and a widow as well. Their Devonshire estate was sold from under them and they've just removed to Upper Wimpole Street. And they are not high flyers!"

Although Lyall was not acquainted with the Coopers he was inclined to agree with his father since no demirep worth her salt would have taken up residence on Upper Wimpole Street, a respectable, but scarcely fashionable section of town.

"I take it the daughters are out of the schoolroom and the widow is hoping to find husbands for them?" Lyall inquired, giving the snuff another try.

"Something like that," the earl said cagily.

"If so, they've arrived at the wrong time," Lyall said, taking the practical view of the matter of launching a female. "It's already near the end of Season with all the balls and routs scheduled far ahead." He shot his father a curious look. "Unless they are trying to inveigle you into sponsoring a gala for them?"

"No, no, nothing of the kind," the earl protested.

"Then I think the better of them," Lyall said. He was still frowning over his open snuffbox. Whatever the point with the Cooper family, he simply did not see why his father should have fallen into a pelter unless...

He paused as he felt himself closing in on the earl's unspoken motives behind his visit. "Do you wish me to arrange something for their amusement?" he asked. "If so you mustn't shy away from asking me. I daresay nothing could be easier to arrange. Perhaps they would enjoy an excursion to Hampton Court or a trip to Madame Tussaud's." He broke off abruptly as he became aware that his father, far from looking pleased by these projected plans, was conducting a rampant search of his coat pockets, which ended with his thrusting a piece of paper at his son.

"You'd best have a look at this," he commanded.

Lyall was by no means sure he should do anything of the sort but, increasingly baffled by his parent's errant behaviour, he picked up the paper, which bore an official-looking stamp. Curious, he held it up to the sun streaming over his shoulder, a negligent smile playing on his lips. But a moment later as his eyes reached the bottom line his smile froze.

"Papa!" he spluttered. "This is a marriage contract!"

"So it is," the earl agreed, walking across to the decanter of Madeira with his son right on his heels.

"But my name is on it!" Lyall wailed.

"I know whose name is on it," the earl replied testily from the sideboard. "That's why I'm here."

"I see. Am I allowed to ask why you waited thirty-two years before informing me of the contract?" Lyall inquired with as much courtesy as he could muster.

"Quite possibly because I forgot all about it," the earl admitted and, seeing the signs of indignation about to sprout anew on his son's face, hastily downed the Madeira.

"Forgot!" Lyall ejaculated. "How could you possibly...?" He found himself suddenly at a loss for words.

By running a finger between his neck and shirt points, the earl managed to avoid his son's accusing eye. "Dash it all, Jeremy. These things happen."

Lyall did not look persuaded by such an argument, and his father made a further attempt at explanation. "I believe Cutter and I reached the agreement one night after a spot of hunting. Can't recall the exact moment it all came about, but I do think we might have been a trifle foxed."

"A trifle!" Lyall roared, regaining his powers of speech. "I should be glad of that, sir. Had you been *truly* foxed I might find myself husband to a dozen wives."

"Oh, not a dozen!" his father protested. "Laws against that sort of thing here, you must know."

Lyall emitted a hollow laugh. "How the devil did you ever remember the contract?" he demanded.

"I told you," the earl retorted. "Miss Cooper. She dug it up and sent me a note asking if it would be convenient for you to call on her at Upper Wimpole Street."

Beads of perspiration dotted Lyall's forehead, which he dried with a handkerchief. "Good Jupiter, can she mean to enforce the contract after all these years?"

To this question the earl shrugged, deeming it impossible to comprehend any female's mind, particularly one neither of them had met.

"Surely the contract cannot be binding," Lyall said, stricken at the notion of matrimony to any female, known or unknown.

The earl waved an impatient hand. "I told you Jarvis looked the contract over, didn't I? No sense getting you into the briars over nothing. But it is valid, my boy!"

Muttering an oath on the betrayal of sons by fathers, Lyall sank into an armchair from which he bleated he could not be expected to marry a female he had never seen before in his life.

"Yes, but that's the whole purpose behind your call on Upper Wimpole Street," the earl said, trying to be helpful. "So you can meet Miss Cooper."

"But I don't wish to meet her!" Lyall declared with rare passion. "Nor wed her, either!"

"It's not necessarily *that* Miss Cooper you might wed," the earl replied gently. "There's a younger sister as well. If you read the contract carefully you'll see it doesn't spell out just which daughter of Cutter's you must marry."

"Unfortunately," Lyall replied, not needing to lay eyes on the hated document a second time, "my name is spelled out all too clearly."

"Why, yes," the earl agreed. "But even if it weren't, everyone in the ton knows that you're my son. And it's not as though you were dangling after someone, or are you?"

"That's not the point, Papa. This marriage contract is! And it's too absurd! Such things are no longer countenanced."

"Perhaps not in your circle," the earl replied placidly. "But it is still done in some places." He paused. "There is just one thing I've neglected to mention. A withdrawal clause comes with the contract."

At these words a flood of relief unloosed itself within Lyall's breast. "A withdrawal clause," he breathed, his brow clearing. "Good heavens, Papa, you should have told me this from the start. I must own you gave me a devil of a fright. I should have suspected that foxed or not, you would never bind me against my will to some unknown female."

The earl fidgeted. "Jeremy—"

His son held up a slender hand. "I know what you are about to say. I fully intend to meet this Miss Cooper of yours."

"Lord, she ain't *mine*." The earl appeared stricken at the very thought. "But Jeremy, you must listen."

"Certainly I shall listen to her," Lyall promised as his mind raced ahead to how soon he could put the matter of Miss Cooper to an end. "I shall be kindness itself," he said, smiling at his father. "I have had considerable experience in dampening the expectations of marriage-minded ladies. I shall look her over and then withdraw gracefully. Upper Wimpole Street, you said? I just hope they aren't dirty dishes."

"It doesn't matter a groat if they are," the earl said crushingly, "since it is Miss Cooper who will do the looking over, not you. The right of withdrawal is hers," he announced and had the satisfaction of seeing his son struck dumb for the second time that morning.

UNAWARE THAT SHE HAD BEEN stigmatized a dirty dish by one of the haut ton's leading members, Davida Cooper sat with her mother and sister in their sitting room on Upper Wimpole Street, her face the only one of the three to betray any sign of dismay over an untidy accumulation of bills gracing the well-worn Pembroke table.

Lady Aldyth Cooper, seated between her daughters with her slender form clad in a lavender walking dress and her blonde hair dressed in a becoming Sappho, gave the pile a negligent glance. At three and forty she had long acquaintanceship with bills and knew how the perusal of sums owed to shopkeepers and modistes inevitably led to a fit of the dismals. An optimist by nature, Lady Aldyth firmly believed that small bills were best ignored and that large ones could be best disposed of with the aid of a sympathetic banker or moneylender.

Miss Cassandra Cooper, on her mother's left, was the youngest of the three ladies and had inherited Lady Aldyth's fair complexion, flaxen hair, and complacency regarding debiture, but at eighteen she could not be faulted too severely for her lack of information on the finer points of finance. An avid reader of lending-library romance novels, she was inclined to view as romantic the possibility of incarceration in a debtors' prison, from which she would be rescued before too uncomfortable a period had passed by her betrothed, Captain Bruce Fitzwilliam, now serving on the Continent.

It was a matter of keen disappointment to Cassie that the family travails were not as yet serious enough to occasion the captain's prompt rescue, or at the very least his return from Spain where he had been posted for the past two years.

Miss Davida Cooper shared none of her sister's fascination with debtors' prisons, being a highly practical young lady of two and twenty. She was also very pretty, with piercing blue eyes which could look askance at any problem rearing its unsightly head, and a mass of raven-coloured curls worn swept back from a heart-shaped face.

Her delicate eyebrows now flew up involuntarily at the sight of the large sum of money owed to Madame Fanchon of Bruton Street. Across the table Lady Aldyth continued to pour tea. Davida sighed, wishing for perhaps the hundredth time that her mother was a trifle less Welsh and able to practise some economies. But this she knew to be an impossibility, as Lady Aldyth treated the mere notion of economy as a novel idea, coming as it did after a solid twenty years of debt and the hovering shadow of foreclosure.

"And it is just that habit of debt," Lady Aldyth had revealed during the actual loss of the family estate a year ago, "that makes all this bearable. Had I not had my long experience of being in debt, I would not know how to contrive!"

Smiling at this memory, Davida laid down Fanchon's bill, her attention having been reclaimed by Lady Aldyth.

"I am certain you will like this tea," her mother was saying. "I bought it from the Berry Brothers, and they claim it came all the way from China, or was it India?" She frowned reflectively before admitting that she could never tell the two countries apart.

"One belongs to us, Mama," Davida answered with a laugh. "The other does not."

"What a simple explanation, my dear," Lady Aldyth said and handed her daughter a cup of the tea, which was every bit as fragrant as Mr. Berry had promised.

"You are up early, Mama," Davida observed.

"An engagement with Mrs. Steele," Lady Aldyth explained. "She and that odious daughter of hers have boxed me into an invitation to Somerset House and I had not the wit to cry off."

"The pictures are alleged to be quite beautiful," Davida said. "But I'm glad I caught you before you set out because I have been meaning to ask you about Fanchon's bill."

"My dear Davida," Lady Aldyth chided gently, "anyone would think you positively business minded to mention such a matter so early in the day. I would never have consented to bring you and Cassie to London had I dreamed you would spend such an inordinate amount of time worrying over debts we have accumulated instead of enjoying yourself."

"I don't worry that much, Mama."

"*Au contraire,*" Lady Aldyth said. "And all for naught, I do assure you. Our creditors have not the least notion that our situation is straitened. But if you insist on paying them off so quickly, they will suspect something is amiss and refuse us credit altogether. I daresay it is your Scottish blood," she added, warming to her topic. "My mother did warn me at the time I was contemplating marriage to your father."

"But, Mama," Cassie interrupted, a biscuit halfway to her mouth, "I am certain that Papa used to tell me it was his mother who warned him against marrying you."

"I daresay you are both correct," Davida said, interrupting what appeared to be a lengthy excursion up both branches of the family tree. "But to return to Fanchon's bill, Mama. I don't mean to pinch at you but two hundred pounds for one dress does seem a bit much."

Lady Aldyth bestowed a smile on her elder daughter. "You may blame Fanchon for that. She is so frightfully expensive, but quite the best in London. And the dress was that sapphire silk I ordered especially to surprise you."

"Yes, Mama, and it was sweet of you."

"For my daughters I would squander a fortune," Lady Aldyth said as her eyes misted softly.

"If you had a fortune," Davida teased. "Just assure me, Mama, that you have no other surprises from Fanchon's for me."

"Certainly not! Haven't you been bending my ear on the importance of making economies? Now, I really would like to sit and chat, but I fear I must go and admire those hideous paintings with Mrs. Steele.'' She kissed her daughters and swept off.

"It is no use talking economy to Mama," Cassie said, as she reached for another biscuit.

"Yes, I know," Davida agreed, gathering up the bills. "And yet I can't help thinking we could try to be more frugal."

"Heavens, we *are* frugal!" Cassie declared. "We've brought only John and Millie with us, and they must be overworked tending the three of us. Not that I mind particularly—" She broke off as they were interrupted by the aforementioned John, who imparted the news that their cousin, Mr. Henry Brakeworth, had called.

No sooner had this name left John's lips than Cassie screwed up her face. "It's a good thing Mama has gone," she hissed to Davida. "I'd wager anything that Cousin Henry is here to deliver another lecture to her."

"You mustn't say such things, Cassie," Davida said automatically.

"Well, I can't abide him, and I don't see how you can. I shan't stay to listen to a word he says."

Davida was no fonder of her mother's cousin than Cassie, and she thought wistfully of making her own escape to an upstairs room, but this would be most uncivil, for in all likelihood Cousin Henry already knew she was in.

With a feeling of foreboding, she moved across the hall towards the parlour. She tried to remind herself that Mr. Brakeworth had done his best to introduce them to his London circle of friends and that he could not be blamed if the circle had consisted mainly of cits and tradesmen.

"Good day, Cousin Henry," Davida said, entering the parlour and almost immediately regretting her words. Mr. Henry Brakeworth stood in the middle of the room radiating gloom from the top of his bald head to the pointed tips of his boots.

"Is your mama in?" Mr. Brakeworth asked, brushing aside her greeting.

"I fear you have just missed her," Davida replied, accepting his rebuff without a qualm. She sat down on the couch. "Might I be of assistance instead?"

Mr. Brakeworth eyed her speculatively. "Do you know what she is up to?"

"At the moment, cousin, I am certain she is bound for Somerset House. An exhibition of paintings, I believe. After that I presume she will return here."

Mr. Brakeworth waved a bony hand. "I don't mean that. I am referring as always to her dreadful gaming!"

Davida bit her lip. Since their arrival in London her mother had fallen into the habit of gaming, and while it was a source of concern for Davida, it had nothing whatever to do with Cousin Henry. "I know you dislike it," she said, "and I do wish she would not, but it is only for chicken stakes."

"If you call ten thousand pounds chicken stakes you are greener than I thought," Mr. Brakeworth said with an audible sniff.

Davida turned to face him, her eyes wide in astonishment at the sum he had just quoted. "Ten thousand, did you say?" she asked, staggered. "She wouldn't!"

"She would and she has," Mr. Brakeworth replied with a gleam of satisfaction as he gazed down his pointed nose at his younger cousin. "And," he added with relish, "she's been covering the loss with loans and has been seen frequenting the cent per centers."

"Moneylenders?" Davida's agitation mounted. "Oh, she wouldn't. You must be mistaken."

"I never make mistakes," Mr. Brakeworth announced with rigid authority. "She was seen headed for the offices of

Messrs. Smith and King. Your mother is a lovely widgeon, Davida. She's been one since the day she was born. But I've come here to tell you she shan't get a farthing from me. I had no notion when I invited all of you to come to London that you would land me in such a dreadful fix."

Davida stiffened. "I am well aware of the debt we owe you, cousin," she answered coldly. "But after all, when my father was alive you often petitioned him for help. On several of those occasions Mama herself interceded with Papa on your behalf. And," she added, "if Papa had not strained the estate lending you considerable sums which were never returned, we might not have lost it."

Mr. Brakeworth looked mollified at these too accurate recollections, but he managed to reply with dignity, saying that the past was the past. "Your father's not alive anymore, more's the pity. And it's not I who's seeking funds these days, but your mama!"

"It is kind of you to acquaint me with the full range of Mama's excesses," Davida said, trying to control her rising temper. "But I recall that she would not be in this fix if you had not introduced her to that odious Mrs. Peel, who lured her into the first of the gaming houses and who, when Mama was woefully behind in her luck, encouraged her to gamble even more to break the streak. And," Davida went on as Mr. Brakeworth looked abashed, "as for petitioning you for help you may rest assured that that will never happen."

"I hope not," Mr. Brakeworth replied grimly. "But just how do you plan to repay her debts?"

"I don't know," Davida replied sharply, "but you needn't fear that we shall hang on your sleeve or put you to the blush! And now you must excuse me for I am very busy this morning."

Hearing the dismissal in her words, Mr. Brakeworth departed, muttering loudly about the ingratitude of relations.

Davida scarcely noticed his departure. Her mind was still reeling from the news her cousin had imparted. Ten thousand pounds! How would they ever contrive to pay off the debt along with all the rest they owed?

CHAPTER TWO

LORD LYALL ARRIVED at Upper Wimpole Street just as Mr. Brakeworth commenced his interview with Davida. His lordship's regard for the unknown Miss Cooper and her family slipped a notch lower while he was forced to cool his heels in a more than modest sitting room, which appeared to have been furnished with the minimum of serviceable furniture, the best of these being a rather lumpy satinwood sofa.

He was coolly surveying it with the help of his quizzing glass when he found himself just as coolly surveyed sans glass by a young lady in the doorway, whose blonde hair was tucked into braids and who wore a pink muslin dress with matching ribbon at her waist. Not in the schoolroom, but not far out of it, he thought, and he put her age at seventeen.

"John says you're Lord Lyall," she declared, stalking in.

A trifle daunted by this unorthodox greeting, Lyall nonetheless admitted to his identity. "Are you Miss Cooper?" he asked faintly, wondering how the sins of his father had passed onto his weary shoulders.

"No," came the encouraging answer. "Davida's occupied at the moment in the parlour. I am her sister, Cassandra, and I should tell you right off, because I hate shams, that I don't wish to marry you and I won't!" Having delivered this pronouncement, she flounced over to the satinwood sofa and glared at him.

"I see," Lyall murmured.

"It's not that I find you wholly detestable," Cassie said, taking this as a sign of good faith. "We have only just met, after all, and I daresay you could be civil. But I am already in love and—" the voice turned mulish "—practically betrothed."

"Practically betrothed," Lyall repeated appreciatively, put in mind now of his niece when she was in high dudgeon. "My felicitations. When may I wish you happy?"

"Whenever Bruce returns," Cassie said, taking this as a sign that he did not intend to press his suit for her hand. "He's a captain on the Continent, you must know."

"France?"

The face before him turned mournful. "Spain. Have you ever been there, my lord?"

"Years ago," he confessed, puzzled by her tragic air. "Why? Are you anxious to go to Spain?"

The tragic expression faded in a trice. "Oh, no!" she burst out. "Davida says it is the most primitive country, and it is hot in all seasons. It's just that I am so eager to have Bruce return. It seems to take an uncommonly long time to return from Spain. Do you think if I told him I were dying of consumption that might induce him to come back sooner?"

"Consumption," Lyall said, controlling his amusement, "might induce your captain to stay away permanently."

"I suppose you are right," Cassie replied after a moment's furious thought, attested to by a furrowed brow and the winding of a ribbon about her forefinger. "I'm so glad you were here to advise me. Do you think that scarlet fever would be the better choice?"

At this new piece of outrageousness Lyall erupted into laughter. "I beg pardon," he said hastily.

"It's all right. You have a nice laugh," Cassie observed. "And I am truly grateful that you didn't turn out to be an April squire or a halfling or a mushroom."

Thinking of his reputation so carefully nurtured, Lyall turned to her now in unveiled astonishment, demanding to know what had induced her to form such an ill opinion of him.

"Nothing, really, but Davida did say we might as well prepare for the worst so that we could be pleasantly surprised if you turned out differently."

"An original approach to life," Lyall murmured.

Cassie beamed with sisterly pride. "Oh, yes, Davida has that. Originality, I mean. Mama claims that always happens when the Welsh meet the Scottish. Blood, you know."

"I take it her Scottish blood is very occupied at the moment?" Lyall inquired.

Cassie nodded. "Cousin Henry," she said in a voice which made plain her opinion of this individual. "He always comes by to read Davida a lecture on what we have done wrong. Fortunately he never stays long, coming only to pinch or scold. And it's highly ridiculous when you consider that Davida is the least extravagant of us all. Mama, I suppose, is the most, and I must be the second, although there is not much a girl my age can be extravagant about, unless she is on the scramble for a husband, which I am not, on account of Bruce."

"So you have mentioned before," Lyall said. His smile turned pensive. "But I wonder if your sister might be, er, on the scramble for a husband."

"Good heavens, no! At least," Cassie said after a moment's careful thought, "I don't think she even cares about marriage, and that is unfortunate because she is quite pretty, and that's why Mama brought us all to London. But what has Mama worried now is that Davida doesn't appear to be enjoying herself."

A door slammed in the corridor. Cassie's face brightened. "That's Cousin Henry on his way out. I told you their talk would not last long, didn't I? I daresay Davida will be quite happy to see you now.''

Anxious to put his interview with Miss Cooper to the test, Lyall accompanied Cassie into the hall and followed her into the parlour.

"Davida?" Cassie called.

"Not now, Cassie," Davida pleaded, without bothering to turn around. "Cousin Henry has just left. And I vow I have never met such a purse squeeze as he. We are in a devil of a coil. And it's no use to tell Mama for she won't pay us any mind."

"But Davida!"

"What is it?" Davida asked, turning in exasperation and beholding in shock not only her sister but the most handsome man she had ever seen. Her gaze took in with mounting chagrin his tall, elegant person, the coat that shrieked of Weston, the pantaloons of the finest biscuit.

"Do not disturb yourself," the image said soothingly. "I can see that you are out of curl. Perhaps it would be better if I returned another day. I'm Lord Lyall, by the way."

"Lord Lyall came in while you were with Cousin Henry," Cassie explained, peering at her sister. "And what did Henry say to make you look so blue?"

"I am not blue," Davida denied, feeling at a distinct disadvantage before someone whose town bronze all but leapt to the eye. "I am merely feeling a trifle angry because of certain, er, things."

"Let me call another day," Lyall suggested again, observing her obvious embarrassment. She was of a different colouring than her sister, with a head of unruly black curls— and, he admitted grudgingly, she was quite beautiful.

"Oh, no," Davida said immediately. If he left he might never come back and then where would they be? "It is all a mull, and I do apologize for greeting you like this, although I had no notion you were coming today. I daresay even if you did return another day an even greater mull might await you."

Rather distracted by his penetrating eyes and feeling dissatisfied by her initial speech to him, which in no way resembled the charming ones she had rehearsed in her imagination, Davida belatedly extended her hand.

"I am Miss Cooper, my lord. I see you are already acquainted with my sister, Cassie."

"Yes," Cassie told her. "And we have got along famously, Davida. He is not at all disturbed to hear I shan't marry him. In fact he took it without a blink."

"Yes," Lyall agreed with only the faintest twitch of his upper lip. "I managed to absorb the blow rather well."

Amusement showed momentarily in Davida's own eyes. Not a dirty dish after all, Lyall thought, and there was something musical and appealing about the voice.

"Do sit down," Davida said, indicating the best chair in the parlour, a sturdy Trafalgar. "And, Cassie, would you mind leaving me alone with Lord Lyall for a few minutes?"

Much to Lyall's surprise Cassie did not protest this obvious dismissal. She flounced out of the parlour, giving her sister what appeared to be a wink.

Davida, intercepting the look of polite inquiry on Lyall's face, wondered if he were already deeming her fast for wanting a word in private with him. Not that it really mattered what he thought of her, as long as he co-operated in her scheme. She took the chair opposite his, hoping that he would not turn out to be an odiously starched-up sort, but she could deduce nothing useful from the civil, faintly quizzical mien he offered for view.

She sat for a moment, wondering how best to begin, when he surprised her by taking the lead, asking if her sister was actually going to wed a soldier in Spain.

"My sister?" She abandoned her scrutiny of the nymphs gracing the painted ceiling. "You mean Cassie?"

"Well, yes," Lyall admitted, hardly relishing the thought that perhaps his father had erred and that there were a possible dozen Miss Coopers all waiting to pass judgement on him.

"I suppose in all likelihood she will wed Captain Fitzwilliam," Davida conceded. "They've known each other from the cradle. But not in Spain if Mama has anything to say about things." She paused, casting a measuring eye over him. "You and Cassie did get along famously, didn't you?"

His smile displayed two rows of dazzling white teeth. "I have every hope that you and I may contrive to do as well."

"Well, I hope so, too," Davida said in a voice that lent no credence to that possibility. "But Cassie and I are quite different. Oh, I am beginning to sound like such a poor creature. I scarcely know how to begin."

"Perhaps I can be of help," Lyall said unflappably, making her wonder if he was so accustomed to females turning hen-witted in his presence.

"This morning I received a visit from my father, the Earl of Exley, who informed me that unbeknownst to me I have been contracted in marriage since birth to a daughter of an old crony of his, now deceased. A copy of the marriage contract had been examined by his solicitor, and since it was held to be binding, I was instructed to dispatch myself at the first opportunity to this residence where I would be duly examined—"

"Examined!" Davida exclaimed. "How abominable that sounds! As though you were nothing but a horse."

Lyall gave her a fleeting smile. "You do not deny you have been looking me over, discreetly to be sure, ever since I entered the parlour."

"I suppose I have," Davida admitted with a rueful laugh. "And I do apologize if it seemed rude, for nothing is more uncivil than for someone to gawk the way all strangers are prone to do at first. And I daresay the news of the marriage contract must have been a dreadful shock to you this morning.''

Lyall, inhaling a pinch of snuff, acknowledged that it had been.

"Then we do have something in common," Davida said with a hopeful ring in her voice. "For it was a considerable shock to me, as well. You have told me how the matter stands from your view, my lord. I should like to tell it from mine."

"By all means," Lyall said, dipping back into his snuff-box and regarding her with what Davida thought of privately as a lord-of-the-manor look.

Davida clasped her hands together in her lap. "I suppose the story begins with my father's death a year and a half ago. Our family estate in Devonshire was foreclosed. That came as no great shock because it was heavily mortgaged. Even so, I suppose we were all accustomed to thinking that in the end everything would come out right.

"Unfortunately Papa had invested quite heavily in the exchange at the wrong time and with frightful results," she said without a trace of self-pity. "After the foreclosure, Mama sold a few of her jewels and we managed to spend a little time visiting our relations. No one was cruel to us," she said, grimacing, "but nor did they welcome us with open arms. I don't know where we might have gone if Cousin Henry hadn't written telling us of this house for rent in London and boasting that he would arrange for us to meet all the right people."

"And have you done so?" Lyall asked, remembering Cassie's opinion of their cousin.

Davida wrinkled up her nose. "Hardly the right sort, my lord. My cousin had led us to believe that he moved in the first circles. That was nothing but a hum. However, as we had already gone to considerable expense to remove here we decided to stay a bit. And I paid a call on Mr. Simon, Papa's solicitor, who had been holding some papers for us. That's when I came across the marriage contract."

At the mention of the contract, Lyall winced. "Yes, the contract is the heart of the matter, is it not? I am curious, Miss Cooper, as to your reaction at the time of the discovery."

Davida shrugged. "I'm certain my reaction matched yours. I thought it a perfect hoax. But Mr. Simon assured me the document was in proper order, and—" she paused delicately for a moment "—it was an opportunity I should not let pass too quickly." When the faint trace of hauteur returned to Lyall's face, she went on hastily, "So I wrote to your father advising him of what I had found and inquiring if it would be convenient to meet you sometime."

"And now you have met me."

"Yes." She gave him another frank look. "Not that I had an expectation of seeing you so soon. And it was civil of you to be so prompt about it. I must also own that I am exceedingly impressed by you!"

Sensing the danger imminent in these kind syllables, Lyall roused himself to take arms against a sea of matrimonial bliss. "Before you become any more impressed by me," he said, coming to his feet, "I should like to say a few words."

"By all means," Davida assured him quickly. "That is why I wished to see you in private, so we might open our budgets and talk freely."

"I hope you won't be too disappointed when I inform you I have no intention of marrying anyone at this stage in my life, particularly one whom I have not met before today. You may be entertaining certain expectations of what life as my wife might entail, and though my position is not as grand as some, it is quite possibly more than you have been accustomed to in the past."

His glance swept meaningfully around the small room. A slow flush rose in Davida's throat.

"You are a lovely young lady," he continued. "And I am quite convinced you will make some gentleman an excellent mate. But I am not he. To be perfectly blunt, Miss Cooper, the idea of matrimony is highly repellent to me. And if you do insist on enforcing this ridiculous document I assure you we shall both be miserable. I'd make a poor husband under any circumstances, and I don't think I'd be a better one if I were leg-shackled to someone wholly against my will."

"But I have no intention of leg-shackling you!" Davida countered. Her voice bristled with indignation at the very idea. "And I certainly have no desire to marry you."

Lyall jerked his head up. "You don't?" he asked, rather stunned by her words.

"I knew if Mama heard about the contract, this was the sort of thing that would result. And that's why I haven't breathed a word to her. It would be a pity to get her hopes up." She gave a wry smile. "You know how mothers can be. I quite assure you, Lord Lyall, I have no wish to marry you."

"I see," Lyall replied, not seeing anything but the plain fact that he had been refused by two ladies in the course of a mere half hour. While he had no wish to marry either, his pride was somewhat bruised.

"Am I to understand that your feelings are engaged?" he asked, seeking a clue for her odd behaviour.

"Why, no," Davida said, surprised into answering what in retrospect was an exceedingly personal question. "It's simply that I could never marry without love, and as I certainly do not love you I could never marry you."

"But, look here," Lyall said bluntly. "If you had no intention of accepting the marriage in the contract, why did you even bother to ask me to call on you?"

Davida coloured under the scrutiny of those cool brown eyes. "Mr. Simon was correct. This was an excellent opportunity, and someone in my position, utterly unknown in

Society, has few such opportunities. I would have to be a gape-seed not to take advantage of it." She paused, noting with a sigh that the arrogant look was back on his face. "I am not in the social circle myself," she went on. "And my cousin's friends are hardly the sort I wish to know better, but you! Your exploits fill the pages of the *Morning Post* and the *Gazette*."

Lyall flushed. "Newspapers have a tendency to overstate things."

"They have not overstated yours," Davida contradicted. "Mr. Simon may be passing fifty, but he is no fool, and he speaks highly of you and the position you command. That's why I have every hope you will be of assistance to me."

Lyall had been listening to her remarks with a polite show of interest, but at the word "assistance," so subtly rendered, he felt a flicker of distaste.

"How much?" he asked as he turned away.

"I beg your pardon?" Davida asked blankly.

"How much money do you want?" he asked impatiently as he faced her. "I know it must be a considerable sum since you have gone to such pains to acquaint yourself with my position." His eyes resembled burning coals. "I congratulate you on your scheme, Miss Cooper. You and your charming sister nearly had me fooled. I shall not scruple to quarrel with you. Money for my freedom would not be too high a price to pay."

"Money? But I don't want your money," Davida declared, the colour now rising in her cheeks.

Lyall frowned. "You did say assistance."

"Yes, help of a sort, but not money. I am not such a grasping female."

He lifted a quizzical eyebrow. "Indeed? I beg pardon. But what other sort of assistance could I render?"

Davida gazed up at him. "I want you to find a husband for my mother," she announced at last.

CHAPTER THREE

"YOU WANT ME TO DO what?" Lyall asked, gaping at Davida.

"Find a husband for my mother," Davida answered promptly. "I suppose you find it a curious request."

"Curious?" Lyall laughed, wondering if it were possible for a young lady to lose her wits in the blink of an eye. And curious would not have been the word he would have chosen to describe her request—absurd, idiotish and freakish being more in the line of things.

"My dear Miss Cooper," he said now, "if you had asked me to jump in the Thames it would have been to more purpose. A husband for your mother!"

"You have not met Mama," Davida said stoutly, "but I assure you she is quite pretty and not so old, being only three and forty and looking at least ten years younger and so pleasant and good-hearted—"

"Seeing you and your sister I would know that your mother's looks would be unquestionable," Lyall said, ruthlessly cutting short this litany of praise. "And I am quite willing to believe she holds all the female virtues to perfection, but that in no way makes me agreeable to your rather eccentric request. I don't mean to be disobliging—"

"But you don't mean to help us," Davida finished for him.

He shifted uncomfortably in his chair. "An elderly matron would be more of a help to you in such a scheme than me."

"Perhaps, but at the moment I am not acquainted with any elderly matrons except for my aunt, who is so under my Cousin Henry's thumb as to be utterly useless, and she turns us the cold shoulder whenever we chance to meet. And as for the men Mama has already met I don't think there is anyone suitable. You must understand I don't wish her to wed just anyone. He must be kind and considerate and a gentleman. I just know that she would suit her position so well."

Although Lyall was a sympathetic listener to these confidences he was in no way persuaded from his earlier adamant position.

"I have no doubt that your mother would acquit herself well in whatever position she held," he said cordially. "But I repeat I cannot help you find a husband for her."

"You mean you don't want to help me find a husband for her," Davida corrected calmly.

Lyall shrugged. Their eyes locked again, and she gave a short nod. "Very well, my lord. We shall have it your way. I'm sorry you have left me no other choice. I had hoped you would co-operate. But I suppose I shall just have to marry you myself."

"Marry me!" Lyall exploded. "My dear Miss Cooper, only minutes ago you were declaring your willingness to perish at the stake before you married without love."

"I doubt I said anything quite so melodramatic," Davida said, unshaken by his accusation. "No doubt you have confused me with Cassie, whose speech does run close to those deplorable novels she insists on reading. While marriage to you will be tiresome, not to mention vexing—for you have made plain the trials any woman married to you will be forced to endure—I shall just have to try and keep myself amused."

Lyall grinned, reading the challenge in her cool blue eyes. "You would do that, wouldn't you?" he said with a dawning respect for her.

"Oh, yes," she declared emphatically. "You must admit that I hold the upper hand in this, and while I should not like to enforce the contract, if need be I shall. I am in earnest about finding Mama a husband. And it's not just a freakish whim, I assure you. I have quite sound reasons for doing so."

"Perhaps your whim is not freakish," Lyall said, "but it is highly original, which now that I think of it your sister Cassie warned me you would be. Most ladies of your years . . . twenty-one?" he hazarded a guess.

"Twenty-two."

". . . are more inclined to be on the catch for husbands themselves than to fall into a pelter about finding one for their mothers."

"Well, I did think of finding a husband for myself," Davida confessed, grinning at the new look of consternation on her companion's brow. "You needn't worry, my lord. I gave up the idea. Even married I would still be obliged to worry about Mama. Plus, I wouldn't be at hand to watch her. You see, Mama is so amiable and kind, and when Papa was living they were so happy. He looked out for her, and while it is true we did not always have money, we were content enough. But now all that has changed. His death came as a great blow to us all, but particularly to Mama. I thought when we came to London she might amuse herself, but she has fallen into certain extravagances."

"Running up bills?" Lyall asked sympathetically, recalling a little of what Cassie had alluded to earlier in the sitting room.

"Much worse," Davida said. "Gaming." She saw Lyall's frown and nodded. "I never dreamed it would come to that. I'm certain she did it only for amusement in the beginning.

Only now, of course, she is so heavily drawn in she cannot possibly extricate herself. And today Cousin Henry brought even more shattering news. Mama's debts have sunk to quite shocking depths.'' She did not dare mention the sum Lady Aldyth owed nor the fact that she had gone to moneylenders. ''That's why it's imperative that I find her a husband, who will take her in hand and look after her.''

''The need for a husband doesn't arise,'' Lyall said briskly. ''If it's the debt that concerns you I can pay it off.''

Davida looked floored at his suggestion. ''But that's impossible. You don't even know Mama. And you can't!''

''Why not?'' Lyall asked, surprised at anyone telling him what he could or could not do.

Several moments passed as Davida struggled to find a reason that precluded accepting Lyall's generous offer. Finally giving up the attempt at rationality she merely said that she would not allow such a thing to come to pass.

''It is one thing to ask a favour of you,'' she pointed out, ''and another to accept money from you. What a toad that should make me, and I would never countenance such a thing.''

Lyall looked at her with some surprise. None of his acquaintances had ever cut up stiff over the offer of funds. Was Miss Cooper's prideful anger mere show?

''Call it a loan,'' he coaxed.

''I shall do no such thing,'' Davida declared with some passion. ''I am not so shabby a creature as to try and lure money from you.''

''And yet,'' he said scornfully, ''you do not hesitate to look for a fortune for your mother.''

''That's different,'' Davida said, colouring slightly. ''Mama herself is no fortune hunter, I assure you. I know I might have painted a lurid picture of her so I shan't blame you entirely for thinking her extravagant or totty-headed, which she is not. But don't you think a few responsible, kindhearted widowers might enjoy their remaining years in the company of a lady like Mama?"

"I do not go through my days with my mind on widowers, Miss Cooper," he replied acidly. A new thought then struck him: "What of you and your sister? Do you go along in the bargain?"

Davida gave her head a vehement shake. The mass of black curls bounced energetically, and he was put in mind of a feisty little terrier shaking himself after a bath.

"There is no danger of that happening. Cassie is quite attached to Captain Fitzwilliam, and once he returns they will marry. As for myself I intend to find a position as a governess in a suitable household."

"A governess?" Lyall ejaculated, amazed at the future she so coolly outlined for herself. "You can't be serious."

"I shall make an excellent governess," Davida stated calmly, well aware of the quizzing look he sent her. Why couldn't he just help them and be done with them? "But my future as a governess does not concern us at the moment. And I rely on you not to tell Mama."

"Governesses are no more my usual conversation fare than widowers," he drawled.

"Nor must Mama know about the marriage contract between us."

"I shan't say a word about that!" he promised swiftly and with good conscience. The fewer who knew about the contract, the better off he'd be. He frowned. If the Bond Street *beaux* got wind of that, he would not be able to show his face in the club for a year! Perhaps he ought to take a hand in Miss Cooper's preposterous scheme.

He gazed across at her and she read the decision in his eyes before he had a chance to voice it.

"You are going to help us!"

Was she a mind reader as well? he mused.

"It might be amusing," he told her as he settled back on the couch. "Now, what did you say you were looking for in the way of a stepfather?"

AN HOUR LATER Lyall drove his Welsh greys away from Upper Wimpole Street and towards White's, where he hoped to discover a widower or two.

A brisk June wind blew, typical of London in the late spring, but Lyall, swathed in his great multicoloured driving cape, scarcely felt it. His mind had been buffeted enough by his encounter with all three Coopers, Lady Aldyth having returned to Upper Wimpole Street in time to make his acquaintance.

Thoughts of the Cooper family, and particularly the elder Miss Cooper, still engrossed him as he stepped through the door of the club, making at once for the reading rooms where it was the habit of the more elderly members to congregate over the afternoon papers to argue politics.

Unnoticed by any of them, Lyall slipped into the room and before long had mentally ticked off the list of deficiencies in the unmarrieds present. Sir Andrew Waugh, warming his hands by the fire, was rich enough to please the mother of Croesus, but he was notoriously bad tempered and would lead any well-bred lady a dance. As for Lord Kingsley, in the corner with his cronies, he suffered from both dyspepsia and gout, and while one might be forgivable, Lyall was convinced that Miss Cooper would frown on a stepfather possessing both.

His glance wandering about the room fell on the Honourable Geoffrey Cunningham, whose good nature was famed throughout London, as was unfortunately his abominably slow wit. In addition, Cunningham was nearly as obese as the Regent himself, and what was worse, he went about entirely uncorseted. He would not do for Lady Aldyth either. Miss Cooper had been strict in her requirements: kindhearted and well pursed, yes, but intelligent and a gentleman of quality, too.

After a mere quarter hour Lyall admitted defeat. There was no way on earth he could broach the topic of matrimony to any bachelor in the room. But if Miss Cooper was serious about her threat to marry him—and there was no foreseeing what a volatile female might do!—it behooved him to consult an expert in matrimonial matters. Fortunately he knew just the person: his sister, Lady Susan Thackerly.

Five years older than her brother, with the same dark eyes and handsome features but with more than twice his energy, Lady Susan resided with her husband on Cavendish Square. She was just stepping out the door when her brother drew up in his phaeton.

"Well, Jeremy," she said, after kissing him fondly on the cheek. "Aren't you going to admire my new walking dress?"

Lyall had already taken in the dazzling red garment Lady Susan had chosen to adorn herself with on this particular day and gave her a polite smile. "Is that what you call it?" he asked, with an interested air. "I would admire it, my dear sister, if it didn't make you look like a robin. Can Walter really encourage you to go out of doors looking like that?!"

Lady Susan's quick laugh rang out. "Yes. And what is the worse, he commissioned it for me entirely without my knowledge, and so I am obliged to wear it. But only on errands where no one is likely to see me. In another month I can give it away."

"If anyone will take it," Lyall said doubtfully. "Are your errands urgent, Sue? I should like advice on a small matter."

"Oh, I can always spare you a few minutes," Lady Susan assured him, and linking her arm through his, drew him into her establishment. She led him into the Crimson Saloon, where her portrait painted by Sir Thomas Lawrence hung on the wall. Over the years both Lady Susan and her portrait had been privileged to hear many of her brother's opinions, but never before had she heard him voice an interest in rich widowers.

"Jeremy, you're bosky!" she exclaimed.

"No, I'm not," he denied. "But I shan't blame you for thinking I've been dipping into the sherry. And I must have put it badly. The matter is urgent, nevertheless. Do you know of any rich widowers? Not—" his voice turned pensive "—that they must be widowers. I daresay any bachelor would do as long as he wasn't deep in the petticoat line."

Incredulity etched itself plainly on Lady Susan's pretty face. "Are you feeling at all the thing?" she demanded, laying one hand on his brow. "The grippe is said to be spreading about town, and I believe you have it. I shall order you a bowl of chicken soup."

"If you do I shall just pour it on your pretty head," Lyall said with brotherly good cheer. "And I don't need bowls of soup. I need a widower; or better yet, two or three."

"Are you planning a collection of them?" Lady Susan inquired in such faint accents that Lyall began to laugh. "How would it be," she suggested, fixing a firm eye on her brother's elegant form sprawled on her Egyptian couch, "if you told me the truth."

"You won't believe it," he warned, but then obediently began the tale.

Lady Susan listened in rapt silence, her list of errands now forgotten.

"A marriage contract between you and this Miss Cooper!" she said breathlessly as her brother came to the end of his story. "Who would have dreamed it of Papa? It's positively gothic!"

"Yes, he must have been foxed. Fortunately, Miss Cooper tells me that nothing will come of it if I am able to find a husband for her mother."

Lady Susan held out a box of bonbons to her brother. "What is she like?" she demanded.

Lyall strove to answer his sister's query. "Three and forty, her daughter tells me, with shiny blonde hair, blue eyes and a kindly disposition.

Lady Susan hurled the candy box onto a buhl table. "Not the mother, you gudgeon," she railed, "the daughter."

Lyall raised an eyebrow briefly at this display of emotion and asked civilly which daughter she was most interested in, pointing out that there were two.

"Whichever is contracted to wed you," she replied, waving a bonbon at him.

"I fear the contract is worded so imperfectly that either may claim me," Lyall reported. "But neither seems inclined to do so at the moment."

Lady Susan, who had been popping bonbons into her mouth in rapid succession, nearly choked at hearing his words. Upon recovery from the coughing fit, which her brother hastened with a vigorous pounding on her back, she demanded to know if he was trying to roast her.

"Indeed not."

"They both refused you?" she asked, staring at him. He nodded.

A broad grin spread on her face. "Well, good for them!"

"Sue," he protested. "You needn't act so gleeful."

"I beg pardon," she replied, looking far from repentant despite his look of annoyance. "But when one considers all the females who are languishing and lying in wait for you to throw them the handkerchief, and these two unknowns profess no interest in you—" Lady Susan broke off into another whoop of laughter.

After a few moments she reclaimed her dignity long enough to inquire what was so lacking in him as a potential spouse.

"The younger Miss Cooper—Cassandra, and quite a delightful creature—is engaged to a captain in Spain," Lyall explained. "And the elder sister is convinced marriage to me would be a fate worse than death. She is willing to make that sacrifice only if all attempts to marry off her mother fail."

"Poor Jeremy." Lady Susan clucked cheerfully. "What a miserable morning you have had; you are quite shown down. No wonder you are distressed. And if the mother should marry successfully? What happens then to Miss Cooper?"

"She intends to become a governess," Lyall reported blandly.

"Good God!" Lady Susan ejaculated.

"I know it is folly," Lyall agreed, "but such is her plan. She's quite foolhardy and wilful enough to attempt such a scheme." He stroked his chin. "Quite possibly by the time we attach the mother to some suitable widower we can also find a husband for Miss Cooper. You shall keep an eye out?"

Lady Susan nodded, and then asked more practically which widowers her brother had in mind for Miss Cooper's mama.

"I don't have anyone in mind," Lyall confessed. "I've just come from White's, and none of the unmarried members there seems likely for a wedding march, which is why I've come here for help." He sat back, observing his sister's coy expression with brotherly revulsion. "And don't look so missish, Sue. It's hardly becoming in a married woman of your years. You know that the one thing you dearly love is to play Cupid. I vow Priscilla was hardly out of her schoolroom and down those stairs before you had her engaged like a shot to Sir William Sidney, who didn't even know what had hit him until he stood at St. George's, Hanover Square, on his wedding day.''

Lady Susan, her face wreathed in smiles at these recollections of her daughter's brilliant match scored two years ago under the very nose of Lady Jersey herself—who had considered Sir William a strong possibility for her third cousin—took issue with only a minor portion of her brother's statement.

''Priscilla was in love with Sir William,'' she reminded him.

''Which made it no challenge for you,'' Lyall answered with aplomb. ''On the other hand I present you with the supreme challenge: an older lady of considerable charm, grace and wit, but without a feather to fly with!''

Lady Susan toyed with another bonbon. ''That would be a challenge,'' she acknowledged, the abstracted air on her face growing more pronounced. ''Why don't you tell me what you can about this Lady Aldyth Cooper?''

Since Lyall's acquaintance with Lady Aldyth dated from only an hour previous, he could offer little substantial information. But Lady Susan had not married off a score of her husband's nieces and cousins as well as her own daughter without a modicum of resourcefulness.

After fifteen minutes of questions exploring the meagre possibilities available so late in the Season, and another five minutes of quite furious thought during which her brother was adjured to be still whenever he ventured a word, she began to laugh.

''What a paperskull I've been. I know of the perfect bachelor for this lady.''

Lyall turned, his sister's Chinese vase in his hand. ''Well, who?'' he demanded.

Her eyes danced. ''Who better than Papa himself?''

CHAPTER FOUR

A BROAD GRIN spread across Lyall's face, a perfect mirror of the impish expression on his sister's.

"By Jove, it would serve him with his own sauce, wouldn't it, to be forced to marry Lady Aldyth!" He slapped his knee with one hand.

"Not force, Jeremy," Susan said firmly as she prudently removed the vase from his grasp. "That would not be at all the thing. We will just allow him time to fall top over heels in love with her."

"That might be asking a bit much of poor Papa," Lyall pointed out. Ever since their mother's death, scores of young beauties had sought to win the attention of the earl, and he had not paid them more than a moment's how-do-you-do. "Lady Jersey claims that Papa was ruined by having Mama as a wife, for there was no way that another could take her place."

"Fiddle! That is romantic babble," Lady Susan said dismissively. "I'm not saying that Mama wasn't wonderful, for she was, but Papa deserves a new life with someone companionable and cheerful. If this Lady Aldyth is all that you say she is, what would be better than to match them? He won't even know what hit him."

Lyall looked at his sister in admiration. "You do work fast, Sue. You've not even seen Lady Aldyth and you are wishing her happy with Papa. If this is any indication of what you can do when you put your mind to it, any bachelor who dares cross your path has my complete pity."

"Oh, this is nothing," Lady Susan said with a wave of her hand. "The real challenge won't come until the day I attempt to find a wife for you! And now do let's try and think of how we can throw Papa in the way of Lady Aldyth."

TRUE TO LADY SUSAN'S PLAN, in the week that followed Lyall found himself furthering his acquaintanceship with the Coopers. He escorted all three about town one morning as they took in the sights of the Tower, which was deemed excessively romantic by Cassie and draughty by Davida, then continued on to Madame Tussaud's famous waxworks.

A luncheon followed, where the younger Miss Cooper, to her mother's distress, displayed an alarming appreciation of strawberry tarts. Lady Aldyth, however, was too good-natured to pay the matter of Cassie's stomach more attention than it deserved. Merely pointing out that Cassie was sure to suffer the stomachache, she settled herself in the carriage for their return to Upper Wimpole Street.

It was a perfect day for a drive. More than once Lyall was obliged to stop and acknowledge the greetings of his acquaintances, who were then introduced to his companions. Being driven about the town in such a fashion by a member of the Four Horse Club was a pleasant experience for any female, but it would have been even more pleasurable for Lady Aldyth if she had been able to determine just how her daughters had made his lordship's acquaintance. Not that she could offer any great protest to his attentions. What mother could object to elegant dress, easy and open manners and a genuine civility? But she did wonder how it all came about.

Besieged by Lady Aldyth's questions on their return home, Davida reminded her of the relationship between the late Mr. Cooper and the Earl of Exley, and with just a little help the pieces fell obediently into place for Lady Aldyth. To further help the pieces fall into place, Lyall asked all the

Coopers to join him at the opera Friday evening to meet his sister and his father. After that invitation excitement was rife in the clan, with Lady Aldyth declaring that her daughters must have new gowns and hang the expense!

"Davida, darling, you have never been to the opera," Lady Aldyth said, turning a deaf ear to her daughter's protests. "Nor has Cassie, come to think of it. And this may be our only opportunity to show you off. You cannot be thinking that, after Lord Lyall has been so kind to us, we can repay his civility by looking like country dowds."

"Oh, no," Davida agreed, blinking at the images her mother had just conjured to mind. "But I do think that the sapphire gown suits me quite well, and since I have worn it only a few times—"

Here Lady Aldyth turned mulish, making pointed objections to her daughters appearing in old gowns, and Davida at last gave in on condition that Lady Aldyth herself commission a new gown.

"But perhaps it is past speaking," Davida said with a laugh, "for Fanchon may not wish to extend us any more credit."

"I do wish you would stop talking of Fanchon," Lady Aldyth implored, reaching into her reticule and silencing her daughter by bringing out a large sheaf of banknotes.

As Davida gaped, Cassie snatched up the money with eager fingers. "Mama, where did this come from?" she asked.

"I have my methods," Lady Aldyth said saucily, unwilling to admit to anyone that she had borrowed twice the sum she had originally intended from Messrs. Smith and King in order to attend finally to the bills Davida had found so distressing. And surely it must have been an act of Providence that she had never gotten round to paying off the debt, for now she could use the money in a much better cause.

"Where did you get the money, Mama?" Davida asked again, fearing the worst.

"A highwayman repented and foisted it upon me," Lady Aldyth said, and that was the only answer she would give Davida as she whisked both daughters off to Bruton Street.

Madame Fanchon, her eyes flashing at the sight of the very cold cash Lady Aldyth—discreetly to be sure—was wielding in her shop, outdid even her own genius. When Lyall appeared on Friday evening, he was greeted by Lady Aldyth in seawater-green satin with a Paisley shawl, Cassie in demure white muslin with matching mameluke sleeves, and Davida in simple blue gauze cut over a tunic of even paler blue gossamer. A sapphire necklace passed down to Davida by her aunt—it being one of the few jewels that had not been pawned during the family's change of fortunes—highlighted her lovely throat.

"You all look splendid," Lyall said as he presented Lady Aldyth with a bouquet of orchids—a rarity in London at any time of the year—which occasioned her prompt squeal of delight. He had not forgotten her daughters, either, offering Davida a sprig of white roses while Cassie received pink. Then he bustled them out to his carriage.

The noted cantatrice, Catalani, was singing that evening at the Royal Italian Opera House, and it was not without difficulty that Lyall manoeuvred his party through the crush into the foyer. There they were met by the Earl of Exley, Lady Susan, and her husband, the Honourable Walter Thackerly, who had dutifully given in to his wife's urgent request for his presence at the opera, a form of entertainment he had never really understood.

Upon meeting the earl, Lady Aldyth fell in with him at once, and the two began a long, mutually satisfactory cose about the late Cutter Cooper. Lady Susan, dressed in a burgundy-coloured gown, which, unlike the red walking dress, had not been commissioned by her beloved husband, took in every detail of the Cooper contingent with interest and approval. Her brother's attention was claimed by Cassie, who was at a loss to understand the Italian in the opera, languages never having been one of her strong suits.

Lyall's appearance in his box with not one but three beauties caused a modest sensation to ripple through the opera house. During the intermission between the first and second acts, Sir Edwin Jeffries, along with that noted of Tulips, Lord Mandley, paid a visit to the box, requesting a prompt introduction to Lyall's charming companions.

Jeffries and Mandley were not the only ones with this intention, as Lyall soon discovered. His box quickly filled with visitors, all flirting in the most outrageous fashion with the Misses Cooper, so that he himself could not get a word in edgewise and was obliged to go out into the corridor, where his sister found him some moments later.

"Good heavens, Jeremy! Here you are, and looking just like Papa used to whenever he was in the sulks. Pray, what is the problem?"

"I am not in the sulks," her brother retorted. "And the problem is I expected to spend a quiet evening at the opera with a few friends and instead I find my box overrun with sprigs and Tulips."

Lady Susan ran her eyes speculatively across her brother's handsome face, repressing a chuckle.

"Don't be such an old woman," she adjured. "You can't mean to hide the Coopers under a bushel, I should hope. Cassie is practically engaged, of course, but Miss Cooper is not. And if she is not in her best looks tonight, heaven help the ladies in the ton when she is. I won't say she has a classical appearance, for her nose is a trifle too short, but when a beauty, particularly an unknown one, appears suddenly everyone is curious."

"I don't object to their curiosity," Lyall said. "It's their curst impertinence." He grimaced. "Did you hear Mandley foisting the most outrageous addresses her way? Everyone knows he's had at least a dozen birds of paradise under his wing since his come-out. And Lord only knows how long ago that was! Moreover, Miss Cooper has been carefully reared in the country.''

"Perhaps, but I don't think you need worry about her," Lady Susan said dampeningly. "She seems eminently capable of taking care of herself."

The success of Lyall's opera party was confirmed the following morning when he called at Upper Wimpole Street, intending to invite Davida and Cassie out for a drive. He found to his great displeasure that this idea, as well as his intended companions, had been usurped by Jeffries and Mandley.

Lady Aldyth, however, was within, and Lyall moved towards the parlour to pay his respects. At the doorway he halted as he found her engrossed in a vigorous tête-à-tête with a morning caller of her own.

It had been Lyall's sincere wish that Lady Aldyth would hit upon a suitable mate at once, but the gentleman with her in no way matched the description Davida had supplied for a stepfather. Mr. Peter Thatcher, only recently turned twenty-three, was a pale, modest-looking specimen in a family whose members all seemed to boast no great vice and no great virtue, being what the Earl of Exley was prone to call a barrel of fish all quite alike.

Surely, Lyall thought, rather daunted at the prospect of such a stepfather for Davida, Lady Aldyth could not be smitten with such a man.

That she was not smitten at all became obvious from the enthusiastic greeting she gave Lyall. He was invited to sit beside her on the couch, and five minutes passed with Mr. Thatcher staring rather pointedly at Lyall and Lyall smiling blandly back.

Thatcher, being the younger, gave in at last and departed, but not before promising to call on Lady Aldyth the following day.

"And I suppose it is rag-mannered of me to hope that he does no such thing," she said after he had gone.

Lyall had been relieved to find nothing remotely lover-like in Mr. Thatcher's remarks to Lady Aldyth and smiled at her now, asking if Thatcher had in some way given her offence.

"Oh, no!" she exclaimed. "Nothing could be further from the truth. In fact, he did me the greatest of favours when I was most in need of it." She lifted up her eyes to Lyall's. "Money," she murmured softly, "but do promise you shall say nothing to Davida."

"I promise," Lyall said, his brow knit slightly at this news. "I take it you owe Mr. Thatcher some money?"

Lady Aldyth nodded as she arranged the remnants of Lyall's orchids in a small vase in front of them. "Yes, and a half-dozen others in London as well. And you must not think that he is hounding me for the money. Quite the contrary." She brooded silently a moment. "In a way I wish he *would* hound me, for then I could be rude and never care if I ever repaid him. But I know he has sustained some very bad losses at Watiers and is himself in dire need of rescue."

Lyall, no stranger to the play at Watiers's green baize tables, was of the opinion that any man as green as Thatcher who ventured into the club would shortly be found in need of rescue.

"Perhaps I could help you, Lady Aldyth."

Lady Aldyth abandoned her brooding to stare at him. "Your help?" she asked. "My dear Lord Lyall, can you be offering me a loan? I would never hear of such a thing. Not," she said, firmly overriding his protest, "when you have already done so much for my family. And never think that I shall forget it. Last night at the opera, for instance—that, I assure you, was worth more to me than mere guineas. The opportunity for my daughters to be seen in such circles is worth far more to me than money," she announced with a flourish and with such an air of finality that Lyall, much as he wished to, did not dare broach the topic to her again.

CHAPTER FIVE

LATER THAT WEEK at a dinner party sponsored by Lady Susan, Lyall had opportunity to observe firsthand Lady Aldyth's gambling. The Coopers had been invited to Cavendish Square along with Exley, and after an excellent dinner including a partridge stuffed with crabmeat, the earl had been persuaded to sit down at the whist table with his son-in-law, Lyall, and Lady Aldyth.

It was intended as just a friendly game of whist but Lady Aldyth's enthusiasm was infectious, and the stakes soon climbed alarmingly from chicken stakes to more than a pound a point, which caused Davida some consternation.

"Mama, I do think you should stop," she whispered in her mother's ear at one point in the evening.

"Oh, Davida, don't be silly!" Lady Aldyth laughed gaily, her face flushed with excitement. "I am having too much fun to stop. Now whose deal is it?" she demanded of her companions at the table.

"Walter is not a Captain Sharp, neither are Lyall or my father," Susan said as Davida resettled herself on the wing-tipped couch. In the seat across from them Cassie thumbed through copies of Lady Susan's fashion magazines.

"Oh, no, I didn't mean to imply that," Davida said immediately. "It's just that Mama and cards are a volatile combination."

"Davida, do look at this drawing." Cassie tugged at her sleeve. "Look at that wig. Wouldn't it be wonderful to wear?"

"It would be dreadfully hot," Davida offered her opinion. "And so heavy to walk with! Who would wear such a thing?"

"I would!" Cassie asserted. "I've always wanted auburn hair, and since you always say that it is foolish to colour my hair, why not a wig?"

"You would look ridiculous," her sister pointed out.

"Cleopatra wore a wig and she had scores of men at her feet."

"You don't need scores of men," Davida retorted. "You have Bruce, remember?"

The thought of her captain restored Cassie's good humour. "I think he'd like to see me in a wig."

"If he ever caught you in one, that would be the last of you!" Davida laughed.

"Let's have some music," Lady Susan interjected, and led the way to the piano. Davida and Cassie followed, and Cassie tried her hand at a few of the compositions she remembered from her lessons. But even as Davida sang along with Lady Susan, she could not keep from worrying about her mother. If only there had not been the invitation to cards. But that was practically impossible. Everywhere they went there was occasion to sit down at cards, except, thank heavens, in church!

By the evening's end her fears were realized. Lady Aldyth's initial winnings were more than offset by her losses, which she paid off cheerfully with a roll of bills that Davida had not seen before.

Where had her mother got the money? Henry's words about moneylenders returned to haunt her. She had to do something about her mother and quickly, she decided that night as she prepared for bed. Lyall, for all his talk about finding widowers for her mother, had done very little to help, though she was obliged that he had introduced them to Lady Susan and Lord Exley.

She tasked him on that point the next morning when he called at Upper Wimpole Street to invite her to drive in the park.

"Instead of taking us for drives in the park or to the opera you should be finding a few eligibles for Mama," she said tartly.

"Patience, Miss Cooper. Or do you want me to drag your mother hither and thither and throw her into the arms of every bachelor of a certain age? They'd think me addled, and they'd wonder what could be wrong with her."

"That is fustian rubbish. You haven't done anything at all to introduce her to any bachelors."

"Oh no? Well, perhaps this will get me out of your black books. A little gift for the three of you!"

"What is it?" she asked as he dropped something into the lap of her cream-coloured muslin.

"Vouchers for Almack's," he retorted, settling his lanky frame into an Etruscan chair, prepared to be showered with thanks.

Great was his astonishment when she thrust the vouchers back at him, adjuring him not to be so stupid in the future.

"Stupid?" One eyebrow lifted in that daunting fashion of his.

Davida was undeterred. "Yes, stupid. Of all the idiotish notions to enter your brain."

"Strange. I never dreamed you would fly into the boughs at the sight of the vouchers. I thought you would enjoy Almack's, and so did Susan. Young ladies have been known to fall into a decline for want of the vouchers. They just languish away."

"Then they must be perfect ninnyhammers."

"They usually are," he agreed complacently. "But what has put you into such a dislike of the place? Or are you afraid of the Patronesses?"

"I am afraid of no one!"

"No, you wouldn't be," he agreed with a smile. How quickly she took umbrage at the idea.

"I don't care about the Patronesses, nor do I care a fig about Almack's. Sir Edwin Jeffries has told me about it."

"Sir Edwin Jeffries?" Lyall gazed at her meaningfully.

She coloured slightly. "Sir Edwin has been calling since you introduced us at the opera. I've learned that Almack's is the marriage mart, patronized by marriage-minded mamas with daughters to marry off, and that the refreshments are mostly stale cakes and sour lemonade!"

"He's right about the cakes," Lyall acknowledged. "But I wouldn't accept everything Jeffries tells you. Does he come here often? I should put a stop to that if I were you. He's a bit of a coxcomb to even think of discussing such things with you."

"I hardly think the frequency of Sir Edwin's calls need concern you," Davida replied in her frostiest manner. "And if he is a coxcomb I wonder why you saw fit to introduce him to me—unless you believe I am in the habit of favouring the company of coxcombs, which I am not. Moreover, the gentlemen to be found at Almack's, I have heard, are usually posturing dandies or fortune hunters!"

"Unfair, Miss Cooper. I have at times gone to the Assembly Rooms and I am neither a dandy nor a fortune hunter. Do remember the mission you charged me with. One way to attract attention to Lady Aldyth is for her to be seen escorting you at Almack's."

"Me?" Davida exclaimed.

"Yes. It would be simpler if *you* appeared to be in the hunt for a suitable husband."

Davida found herself nearly bereft of speech. "In the hunt! For a hus..."

"Husband," he said with a smile. "Splendid plan, don't you think?"

"It is outrageous, abominable—"

"Listen to me," he said, cutting into her criticism. "As you move about London, so will your mama. Her gaiety and charm will become evident to the more discerning bachelors. And lest your role seem too arduous you could always practise throwing out your lures with me."

"It's not a lure I'd wish you, Lyall."

"Yes, I know." His eyes danced. "You'd sooner wish me to Jericho. But you will like Almack's, and so will Cassie. And it is for your mama's sake. She is a remarkable woman, and she plays her cards well for a woman. Of course, the luck was against her last night. That reminds me that I wished to return this." He dug into the pocket of his coat.

"What is this?" she demanded as he held out an object toward her. "Money?"

"Unless you wish to use it as jewellery," he pointed out, as she held up a gold crown to him in astonishment. "I admit the Egyptian craze is very strong in London, and the Egyptians were in the habit of wearing coins as jewellery, but I daresay if you started to do so you would look nearly as freakish as Cassie in that wig she wants to buy."

"But why are you giving me money?"

"Because if I returned it to Lady Aldyth she would just toss it onto another card table," he said with a sigh. "I never gamble for such high stakes in my sister's drawing room."

"You needn't explain," she said. "Mama raised the stakes. I heard her myself. And this money is yours." She attempted to give it back to him, but found her every effort to do so rebuffed.

"Don't be so quarrelsome about it," he declared. "If you don't take it, I shall just give it to Lady Aldyth, who will gamble it away, or to Cassie, who will invest in a wig! You seem the most sensible one of the three who live under this roof."

This was the most left-handed compliment she had ever received, but there could be no denying the truth in it. She didn't wish to accept anything from him, but the memory of the pressing bills to pay bade her accept his generosity.

"Very well. I thank you."

"That wasn't so hard, was it? Thanking me," he said in answer to her questioning eyes.

What an infuriating man he was, Davida thought later after Lyall had departed. Thank him indeed. She would be heartily glad when she saw the last of him.

"VOUCHERS FOR ALMACK'S, where did you get them?" Aldyth asked when she and Cassie returned from their morning calls an hour later.

"Lyall brought them."

"This is a plum I didn't expect to fall our way," Lady Aldyth said, examining the vouchers. "But perhaps Lyall has a special reason for wanting you there," she added with a mischievous glint in her eyes.

Davida stared at her mother in utter bafflement. "What do you mean, Mama?"

"I mean that he has showed us all round London, introduced us to his father and sister and now presents us with vouchers. I have cut my wisdoms. You have an admirer, my dear."

Davida swallowed a whoop of laughter. "You mistake his feelings. I assure you there is nothing loverlike in his behaviour with me," she said finally.

Lady Aldyth patted her on the cheek. "He doesn't wish to raise expectations. You must know that he has half the ladies of the ton languishing after him."

And what a hen-witted brood they must be, Davida thought, but did not voice this contrary thought.

"Will you come to Almack's with us, Mama?" she asked.

"Why, yes," Aldyth said, a bit surprised by this request. Her elder daughter was usually so self-assured. Was it possible that she was daunted by the Assembly Rooms?

"Don't fall into a pelter about things, my dear," she said, squeezing Davida's hand. "I shall endure the prattle of the Patronesses in order to see you happy." She clasped her daughter to her bosom briefly. "To see you happy, what is a little boredom?" Swaying in tune to an imaginary Strauss waltz, she swept up the stairs.

"I shan't need my voucher," Cassie said, dipping into the bag of peppermints she had bought during her outing with her mother. "I am practically betrothed to Bruce."

"You *must* come with me, Cassie," Davida said. "If I am to be in the hunt for a husband, I may be too distracted to keep a sensible eye out for a widower for Mama. You must help me."

Cassie sucked noisily on the peppermint. "In the hunt for a husband? I thought you said such actions were hurly-burly, leading gentlemen to think a female hoydenish."

"Yes, I know and I do. Don't be idiotish. It's Lyall, of course. See what he has brought me to!"

"Well, if you want Lyall," Cassie replied, not seeing what the fuss was all about, "you have only to enforce the contract!"

"I don't want Lyall," Davida said vehemently. "I can think of no one who would suit me worse. All I want is to get Mama happily married to someone reasonably good-natured. It is Lyall's idea to pretend that I am interested in a husband. Mama will accompany me about and show herself off to advantage."

Cassie frowned. "It's a pity about your not wanting Lyall. I'd wager a dozen females would love to get their hands on him. He is considered a veritable swell."

"Don't be vulgar," Davida implored, beginning to get a headache from all this talk of Lyall. "And don't let's sit talking about him. I am going to choose my dress for Almack's. Are you coming?"

"Later, perhaps," Cassie answered. "I am finishing a letter to Bruce." She heaved a sigh and Davida looked across with quick concern. It was not characteristic of Cassie to look so downcast.

"What's wrong, pet?"

"Bruce," Cassie replied.

"You miss him?"

"More than I thought possible. And he hasn't written in weeks, not even when I wrote to tell him I had the scarlet fever."

"You told him what?" Davida asked faintly.

"I did that so he would hurry back, of course," Cassie explained. "But you see what kind of man he is. With his betrothed dying of scarlet fever he is still dallying with his Spanish ladies."

"You are not dying of scarlet fever," Davida said briskly, wishing her sister had paid one less visit to Hookam's lending library. "And Bruce is not dallying with any Spanish ladies. If he hasn't answered you it's because the mail to the peninsula is slow. And," she reminded her sister, "he loves you."

"Yes, I know. But it is so hard to wait for him," Cassie said, picking up her quill again.

Minutes later she tore up the letter she had been writing. Bruce already knew how much she missed him and didn't seem to care a jot. What she needed was another way to get him to come home. What if he thought she was enjoying herself enormously in London in the company of a charming and handsome young man?

She sharpened another quill, thinking hard. If Bruce thought she was going to marry someone else, that might bring him home on the run. Turning this excellent plan over in her mind for several minutes, she perceived only one tiny flaw. The only gentleman she knew was Lyall. But surely, she thought as she began to scribble furiously, his lordship would not mind being betrothed to her just in a letter, particularly since she had no intention of holding him to it!

CHAPTER SIX

GETTING THE COOPERS to Almack's was a far easier task than inducing Exley to set foot there. Lyall, declaring the matter totally beyond his capability, took the cowardly way out, delegating the task to Lady Susan.

"Papa hasn't been near the Assembly Rooms in at least a decade," he explained to his sister. "I am at a complete loss how to get him there now."

"Your trouble, Jeremy, is that you have no imagination," Susan remarked, cutting the thread off the embroidery she had just finished stitching. "How does that look?" She held it up for her brother to admire.

"Fine, if you like birds," he said, examining it and then putting it down when he realized what he was doing. "Pray stop admiring your stitchery and attend to this matter. It will need every ounce of imagination you possess to concoct some way of getting Papa to King Street Wednesday night."

"Oh, it shan't be that difficult," his sister said airily, putting her scissors back in the box.

Lyall found her serene expression nettlesome. "Would you care to wager on that?" he asked.

"With the greatest of pleasure."

"If I win," Lyall said without hesitation, "I'd fancy a bottle of that excellent vintage claret Walter served us the other night."

"And if I win," Susan said, "you must let me drive that high-perched phaeton of yours!"

This condition took Lyall aback. Ordinarily he allowed no one except his groom and himself to handle his vehicles. But there was little likelihood that Susan would win the wager.

On Wednesday evening Lyall strolled into the Assembly Rooms, taking his place amid the other gentlemen of fashion, whose number included, he discovered, the Earl of Exley.

He lost not a second in finding his sister, detaching her from a contingent of Patronesses. "How the devil did you do it?" he demanded.

"Lord Timothy Fife."

"What?"

"He owns the bay that dear Papa has been pining to buy. But he would never listen to any of Papa's offers."

"What has a *horse* to do with the Assembly?" Lyall said thickly, on the verge of strangling his sister.

"Lord Timothy's daughter is coming out this season. Like the dutiful father he is, Fife is keeping an eye on the sprigs who are paying their addresses to her. So he is in attendance this evening."

"I see." The light dawned at last.

"And I think that I shall drive your carriage tomorrow in the park."

"Fine. I shall bring it around at ten for our drive."

"*Our* drive? Unfair!" she protested.

"You don't think that I will allow you to drive my vehicle by yourself."

"You wagered."

"You asked to be allowed to drive my vehicle. Nothing was said about being alone."

"Oh, very well," she said, giving in with a laugh. "Now, do you think Papa will dance with Lady Aldyth?"

Involuntarily Lyall's eyes sought out the lady in question, who was looking quite gay in a periwinkle-blue watered silk. Davida, lovely in rose-coloured satin, was talking to Sir Edwin Jeffries, and Lyall toyed with the idea of asking her for a dance.

But before he could do so, he found Cassie at his elbow, and the chit prevailed on him to partner her in the waltz. Was such high-handed behaviour an ingrained Cooper trait or had the girls learned it from the cradle?

"I have something to say to you," she said breathlessly.

"So I perceive from that pensive look on your face," Lyall answered warily. "What is it this time?"

"I told Bruce I was being forced to marry you," Cassie said, deciding to make a clean breast of it.

Lyall nearly trod on her foot. "You told him what?" he thundered.

"Not so loud," Cassie pleaded, nodding at Davida who was dancing now with Major Gardiner, and looking none too pleased to see Lyall partnering her sister. "Davida might hear you."

"What kind of gibberish are you handing me, you abominable brat? You are not being forced to wed me."

"I know that," Cassie answered. "But I still don't see why you should be so vexed. It's not as though you are planning an engagement of your own. Or are you?" She paused, but Lyall thought better than to answer such a besotted question. "And anyway I had to do something. It's just temporary, to get him back to London!"

"When in all likelihood he will run a sword through me," Lyall prophesied gloomily.

"I shan't let him do such a thing," Cassie promised. "Besides, I don't think he uses a sword."

"Unfortunately," Lyall pointed out, torn between amusement and anger, "in the heat of the moment your captain may not choose to hear anything you say. And who can really blame him, for you have been telling the most atrocious untruths. Does your sister know of your plans?"

"Oh, no, she'd never approve of such a scheme. But I had to do something," Cassie said, hanging her head and looking so forlorn in her yellow ball gown that the lecture Lyall had been about to deliver on the unsuitable habit of embroiling perfectly innocent gentlemen in her schemes withered on his tongue.

"I take it the bout of scarlet fever didn't turn the trick?" he asked in a gentle voice.

"No," Cassie said miserably. "And I do miss Bruce so terribly."

"What will you do when your captain arrives? You don't intend to marry me, do you?"

"Oh, no. I have it all arranged. You shall just say you have changed your mind. That way, no one but the three of us need ever know. And I shall swear Bruce to secrecy." She paused. "Although it might be more dramatic if you shed a tear or two as you relinquished my hand."

Lyall gave a shout of laughter, which drew some stares from the others dancing around them. "You are a minx, my girl! And I am not about to wear the willow for any lady, especially not a chit like you! I'm more inclined to banish you to your room if you ever do such an outrageous thing again. If your captain does show his face in London and does not immediately run me through, you shall tell him the truth, is that understood?"

"If you insist."

"I do," he said as the waltz ended. He returned Cassie to a chair near his sister and discovered Davida shaking hands with one of his old friends, Mr. Hugh Sylvester, recently returned from the Continent, where he had been posted in service to Wellington.

"Hugh, how are you?" he asked.

Mr. Sylvester, a pleasant, fair-haired gentleman, smiled at him as they shook hands. "Very well, Jeremy. I was just telling your friends that had I known Almack's boasted such lovely ladies I would have visited more often.''

"If Wellington could have spared you," Lyall pointed out.

"Hugh is in the diplomatic field," Lady Susan explained to Davida and Cassie. "At least he was. The duke has given him leave to return."

Davida smiled. "London must seem dull to you, sir, after all you have encountered on the Continent."

"Not in the least," Hugh answered promptly. "Perhaps you will allow me to tell you a bit about the Continent." With a polite smile at Lyall and Lady Susan he moved off with Davida, trailed by Cassie, who was yearning to ask if he had ever been to Spain and happened on one Captain Bruce Fitzwilliam.

Lyall watched them go with a frown. "Four years on the Continent have turned Hugh rude, I must say."

Lady Susan sighed. "He wasn't rude, Jeremy, merely anxious. Anxious to know Davida better. And who can blame him? He has known *us* all his life."

"But I don't see why he should be particularly anxious to meet Davida," Lyall complained.

Lady Susan gave a heartfelt sigh. "Sometimes, Jeremy, you can be such a nodcock."

Lyall, on the verge of uttering a blistering retort, swallowed it as Lady Aldyth drifted up.

"Lord Lyall, the very one I have been searching for. Thank you so much for procuring the vouchers for us."

"It was nothing, I assure you, Lady Aldyth."

"General Cathcart looked quite enchanted with you, Lady Aldyth," Susan teased. "I vow, after your dance with him, he demanded to know all the particulars about you from Lady Jersey."

Lady Aldyth laughed and fanned herself. "When a man reaches a certain age, one I'm certain the general has reached long ago, he can be enchanted by anything that moves as slowly as he does.''

''Viscount Bowlin seems anxious to dance with you.''

''Yes, I know. He's asked me for one. But I have had my fill of dancing. I'd liefer play cards. I was just about to go to the card room.''

''No, you mustn't,'' Lyall said. ''I mean, I think my father would like to dance with you. Wasn't he saying as much, Sue?''

''Yes, indeed.'' Lady Susan lent her weight to that scheme. ''You will allow him that honour, I hope?''

''Yes, of course. But I don't see him here.''

''I do,'' Lyall said, his greater height allowing him to see his father across the room, deep in discussion with Lord Timothy concerning the bay.

''Five hundred pounds, you can't ask for anything more than that,'' the earl was declaring as his son drew closer.

''Not for sale, Exley, I vow. Don't you ever listen?''

''Papa,'' Lyall interrupted. ''May I have a word with you?''

''Not now, Jeremy,'' the earl said, but it was too late. Lord Timothy, taking advantage of Lyall's presence, had swiftly retreated. ''If I lose that bay it will be your fault!'' the earl chided.

''I don't think Timothy will part with it.''

Exley snorted. ''What do you want?''

''Lady Aldyth was desirous of a dance with you,'' Lyall said, leading his father back across the ballroom.

Exley came to a rigid halt. ''What? Dance? Me? I haven't danced in years.''

''That doesn't matter. It's not one of these new-fangled steps, I assure you; merely a set of country dances,'' his son encouraged him.

''Oh, I say, Jeremy, she can't mean it. I never was very good at dancing,'' Exley said in real terror.

"You will be fine," Lyall assured his parent, pulling him over to Lady Aldyth. "Here is your partner at last."

With an agreeable smile Aldyth took the earl's arm.

Lady Susan's eyes twinkled happily. "Nice work, Jer."

"Poor Papa looks terrified."

"Yes, doesn't he," she agreed, chuckling warmly. "And everyone has noticed he is dancing." Everyone included the Countess Lieven, Maria Sefton, Lady Jersey, and Lady Aldyth's two daughters.

Davida, sipping some champagne with Hugh, listened indulgently to the flow of diplomatic intrigue he dropped in her ear. Now and then, however, she was forced to abandon him and Wellington in the middle of a crisis as her eyes followed her mother across the ballroom floor. When the dance ended, Viscount Bowlin prevailed on Lady Aldyth for a dance, and then General Cathcart led her off.

"Your mother has made a notable hit here," Hugh observed.

"It does seem that they are taken with her."

"And it would seem that Lady Aldyth's charms run in her family."

Davida coloured, but accepted his homage with light-hearted ease. "You have been away, Mr. Sylvester, so perhaps you are unaware that a gentleman does not say such gallant things to a lady while she is drinking champagne. It might cause her to choke."

"It would not cause you to choke, Miss Cooper," Hugh replied with aplomb, "since you are probably accustomed to hearing such compliments."

This made Davida laugh, and her outburst caused Lyall, standing a few yards away, to look up frowning, which made Davida quite irrationally laugh twice as hard at Hugh's next sally. Had Mr. Sylvester been a more self-centred gentleman he might have fancied himself turning into a wit.

The evening passed in a comfortable fashion. Davida, who had not expected to enjoy herself, found she became caught up in the lights and excitement of the assembly. The ladies so beautifully gowned, the men so handsome, and even the much maligned refreshments were part of a night she would never forget. So absorbed was she that she lost track of her mother, and it was not until the end of the ball when she and Cassie were searching for her that they discovered Lady Aldyth in the card room.

"Oh, no!" Davida ejaculated. How could she have been so remiss in her duties?

Lady Aldyth, however, laughed off Davida's worries. "You couldn't expect me to dance the whole evening," she pointed out. "And I saw no reason to be a chaperon since you were doing so splendidly. Did you dance with Lyall, my dear?"

"No!" Davida replied brusquely. This was one sore point to her evening. Why had Lyall danced with Cassie and not with her? He was just being vexatious. Not that she would have agreed to the dance if he had asked.

"Mama, pray do not change the subject. How much did you lose?"

"Oh, Davida, do stop worrying, my dear. No one has dunned me yet," she said cheerfully, and would not say another word despite her daughter's entreaties.

CHAPTER SEVEN

ON THURSDAY MORNING Lord Exley strolled into the reading rooms of White's, still fretting over Lord Timothy's intransigent behaviour of the night before. The earl did not consider himself a stubborn man, but he had his heart set on the bay, and it vexed him beyond belief not to be able to add it to his stable.

He nodded to a half-dozen acquaintances, then settled down in a sturdy Trafalgar chair to peruse the daily papers. It was his custom at this hour of the day to spend his time reviewing the political scene in Vienna, but today the earl found his morning ritual broken by members who came in to quiz him about Lady Aldyth Cooper.

"Such a pretty pair you made as you danced with her last evening," Philip Forbish, one of the bow-window set, said with a titter.

Exley frowned. Forbish was a popinjay given to vividly coloured waistcoats.

"What are you speaking about?" he demanded.

Forbish polished his quizzing glass with a lavender handkerchief. "A widow and a widower seem a convenient match to me," the dandy mocked.

"What the devil are you prattling about?"

"Let me be the first to wish you happy," Lord Linley, one of Forbish's cronies, interjected.

"Be off with the pair of you," Exley roared. "Puppies! Impudent pasty-faced brats!" he shouted as the two dandies fled laughing, appearing not to notice a tall grey-haired gentleman standing squarely in their path.

Since he did not wish to be trampled underfoot, the gentleman gave way to the dandies, and turned to see who had routed them from the reading room.

"In a bad temper, George?" he inquired.

The earl scowled and turned, ready to do battle with another young sprig. Instead he found his old friend, the Marquis of Alwyn, grinning at him.

At once his scowl vanished. "By Jove, Alwyn, where did you come from?"

"Across the Irish Sea," Alwyn replied, shaking hands with his friend. "I'm in town for a fortnight. Staying at the Connaught."

"What, a hotel? Stuff and nonsense," the earl protested. "You'll stay with me at St. James's Square. What brings you in? Thought you'd sworn off England as a mere nation of shopkeepers!"

"Those words belonged to Napoleon, not me!" Alwyn said with a twinkle in his blue eyes. "In truth, I'm thinking of purchasing some new bloodstock for my stables. Do you know of anything good hereabouts?"

"Fife has some capital stock," Exley said gloomily, reminded of the bay that he still wanted. "But he won't sell. Or at least he won't sell to me." Over a glass of claret the earl confided to Alwyn his trouble with Lord Timothy. "I told him to name his price. Even went to Almack's last night. Waste of time."

"Almack's!" Alwyn cocked his head at the earl. "I can scarcely credit such a tale. Did you really go to Almack's?"

"Aye," Exley admitted. "And I wish I hadn't, for not only did I not get the bay I wanted from Timothy, it has given rise to the most idiotish stories."

"About the bay?" Alwyn asked, in some confusion.

"No... It's deuced complicated—" the earl began, then broke off abruptly as Forbish returned to the reading room.

"What do you want?" he demanded.

"Excuse me, Lord Exley," the dandy said with a smirk, "but I thought you might want to know that the odds on your winning the hand of Lady Aldyth are in your favour!"

"Odds? Do you mean it's in the betting book?" Exley thundered. He stormed out of the reading room followed closely by the marquis, who peered over his shoulder when the betting book was examined.

"Damn puppies!" the earl fumed. "Wagers on me, indeed!" He slammed the book shut.

"Who is Lady Aldyth Cooper?" Alwyn asked calmly, following his friend out of the club.

"No one," Exley replied, jabbing his cane into the street. "And certainly no one I should wish to marry!"

A look of comprehension passed across Alwyn's face. "Oh, I see. One of that sort."

Exley stopped in his tracks. "Oh, bless me, no. She's not a cyprian. She's a perfectly respectable and amiable widow. Widow of Cutter Cooper, do you remember him? No, I daresay you don't. You were a year younger. But I'm not going to marry anyone," he roared. "Wager or no wagers!"

THE PAYMENT of a different sort of wager occupied the earl's offspring that same morning, as a certain high-perched phaeton took the turn in the park rather too briskly to suit its owner.

"Will you be careful, Sue? That's the fourth time you nearly ditched us!" Lyall said, laying a restraining hand on the reins.

"Stop being an old woman, Jeremy," Susan retorted cheerfully, her face flushed with the exertion of keeping her brother's prized Welshbreds in hand. "I'm supposed to be doing the driving."

"You'll drive us into an early grave if you're not careful. Watch out!" he exclaimed as the carriage nearly collided with a solitary rider, whose horse reared back just in the nick of time.

"Oh, for goodness' sake!" Lady Susan expostulated, thrusting the reins at her brother. "How can anyone drive with you twitching in fear beside her?"

"I have never twitched in my life," he retorted, but gladly accepted the reins.

"I'm sorry, Sue," he said finally after a few minutes of stony silence spent rounding the Serpentine. "I'm deuced particular about my vehicles."

Lady Susan bestowed a forgiving smile on him. "Well, I'm obliged to admit that your vehicle is a bit more difficult to manoeuvre than I had thought. I shall have to be content with my barouche." They finished the turn about the park, and Lyall consented to stop at Hookam's, for Susan was in dire need of reading material.

"All Walter has are those ridiculous pamphlets about landscaping," she explained to her brother as they entered the shop. "Why, Hugh!" she exclaimed in surprise as they came upon Mr. Sylvester.

Lyall shared his sister's shock. In no way could Mr. Sylvester be considered one who enjoyed reading.

"Good morning, Susan, Jeremy," Hugh said cheerfully.

"Hugh? Good Jupiter, I didn't think it were possible."

"That's a fine greeting, I must say."

"I beg pardon, but I hardly imagined that I would be exchanging social niceties with you over a table of books! You are the one who once told me you could not see what the fuss and botheration was over Byron's work, and yet there you stand with *Childe Harold* in hand."

"Is that what it is?" Mr. Sylvester looked down uneasily at the volume he carried. "Actually, I'm holding it for Miss Cooper."

"Indeed?" Lyall said.

"Yes," said Miss Cooper, emerging from behind a bookshelf. She wore a white walking dress, an unwise choice, as she freely admitted, since the bookstore was so dusty. "But then I didn't think we would come here when Mr. Sylvester invited us for a drive."

"Us? Do you mean your mother?" Lady Susan asked.

"No. Mama is still asleep. Cassie came with us. She begged Hugh to stop here, and he was too good-natured to say no. She is perusing the novels, I believe. Let me take my Byron, Mr. Sylvester."

"Not until I pay for it," Hugh insisted and overrode her protests, going off to find a clerk to make the purchase.

"I didn't expect to find you up and about so early this morning," Lyall said, watching Davida rub at a dust spot on the sleeve of her dress. "After last night I fully expected that you would sleep late."

"You are up early yourself," she pointed out, giving up on the smudge.

"Yes. I had promised Susan to drive with her in the park."

"That's where we were headed before Cassie asked Hugh to stop here. She is thoroughly addicted to those romances she reads."

His lip twitched. "Do you disapprove of all novels, Miss Cooper, or just romances?"

She considered the question carefully. "Some novels have merit. Miss Austen's, for instance. But the majority lack skill and insight. And romances are the worst!" She glanced up at him. "Have you ever read one?"

"No," he admitted.

"You have not missed anything. The heroines are invariably so insipid I could scream. And the gentlemen are the haughtiest creatures imaginable. Why either would fall in love with the other is beyond my comprehension."

"Spoken like someone who has never been in love," he said, looking at her a trifle too closely for her comfort. "Would you rather they came to grief?"

"It would make for a more interesting book," she answered and, wondering if she ought to be insulted by his comment on her never having been in love, turned as Cassie approached with her arms laden with books.

"Cassie! You cannot buy all of those."

"They are mine," Susan said cheerfully. "I invited Cassie to read those that she likes and return them to me when she finishes."

Since Lady Susan's gesture was a kind one, Davida could not really protest too much. Hugh gallantly volunteered to carry the heavy load of books. He made a rather besotted beast of burden, in Lyall's opinion, particularly with that mooncalf look on his face.

"Why are you frowning at me, Jeremy?" Hugh asked as they followed the ladies toward a nearby milliner's shop.

"I suppose it is just the nauseating spectacle of you dangling after Miss Cooper."

Hugh laughed away the insult. "Can that be the green-eyed monster talking?"

"Good heavens, no."

"Good. For I hope soon to claim her as my own." With a pointed elbow he nudged his friend aside as they went through the door of the milliner's shop.

Cassie, absorbed in a choice of ribbons for a hat she was hoping to refurbish, happened to glance up just then and saw the black look crossing Lyall's usually benevolent face. The expression grew even more pronounced, she noticed, whenever he looked Hugh's way and reminded Cassie rather forcibly of the description in *Lady Pamela's Betrothed*, when the Duke of Armandy had spied a foe for Lady Pamela's hand. Of course Lyall was not a duke, she told herself, and there was nothing for him to be jealous of, unless— and here she nearly pulled the roll of ribbon off the counter—he were jealous of Hugh, over Davida!

Not for nothing had Cassie consumed one romance daily since their arrival in London, and she quickly abandoned the ribbon, to pursue her thoughts. Later, in the carriage on the way back to Upper Wimpole Street, she scrutinized Hugh and Davida, satisfying herself that while Hugh appeared to be dangling after Davida, her sister did not seem in the throes of a grand passion.

If there had been a true romance budding between the two, Cassie would have thought twice before interfering, but she had no scruples now. True, Hugh was handsome and friendly, but so was Lyall. And they had known Lyall longer. While it was civil of Hugh to drive her to Hookam's, Lyall had also taken them for trips, including the outing for strawberry tarts.

It was the strawberry tarts that tipped the scales in Lyall's favour, as far as Cassie was concerned.

After their return to Upper Wimpole Street, Hugh drove off, and Cassie attempted to speak to Davida about Lyall. But Davida was preoccupied.

"I must wash off this stain on my dress before it sets, and then I must see how much Mama lost in the card room."

It was no use, Cassie decided; Davida would not listen. What elder sister had ever listened to a younger one? But if Cassie waited for Lyall to cease his thunderous looks and do something useful, such as to sweep Davida onto his saddle, it could take forever. He struck Cassie as thoroughly lacking in any kind of imagination.

Fortunately she was here, and thanks to her extensive reading in the field of romance, the situation was quite elementary. She would take a hand in things, help Lyall fight off the interloping Hugh and win Davida's hand.

UPSTAIRS THE OTHER TWO Cooper women sat on a daybed together.

"How was your drive with Hugh?" Lady Aldyth asked, recognizing all the signs that Davida was out to have a serious discussion with her about her finances, and determined to do her best not to have it.

"I do believe that if Lord Lyall is not careful, Mr. Sylvester will steal a march on him!" she went on, and scored a hit as Davida went off on this tangent.

"Mama, really!" she protested. "I scarcely think that one drive is a declaration."

Lady Aldyth put down her tambour frame. "Oh, it is early days yet," she agreed. "And there's many a slip 'twixt the cup and the lip, as the saying goes. But at least Hugh is an improvement on Sir Edwin. I know I shouldn't be uncharitable, but I've never had much patience with quacks."

"Sir Edwin is not a quack. He just has a delicate constitution."

"I have never met a quack who had a robust constitution," Lady Aldyth drawled.

The mention of Sir Edwin was a mistake, however, for Davida had no interest in the baronet and returned to the purpose of her tête-à-tête with her mother.

"How much did you lose last night at Almack's?"

"Now, Davida, I hate to scold, but you are turning into a dead bore on the topic of my gaming debts."

"Mama, I don't mean to."

"I know you don't. I assure you, it is the merest trifle, easily dispatched. Why, last night Lord Hennessey was more than happy to accept my vowels."

"And how will you pay off the debt to Hennessey, as you must eventually?"

"Yes, eventually everything must come to pass," Lady Aldyth said. "Hennessey, however, will have to wait his turn. I should pay off Mr. Thatcher first."

Davida had been unaware that her mother owed anything to Mr. Thatcher. How many other creditors did she have? Davida could not help the urge to shake her wayward parent.

"Oh, dear, I shouldn't have told you about Mr. Thatcher or Lord Hennessey. It just upsets you so."

"Doesn't it upset you, Mama?" Davida asked, wondering at the cheerful expression on her mother's face.

"Heavens, no. I shall find a way to pay off Mr. Thatcher. He hasn't been pressing me this week. And after I pay off Mr. Thatcher I shall pay off Lord Hennessey." She bestowed a radiant smile on her daughter.

Was there no hope for her mother? Davida wondered, close to despair. "You'll go to the moneylenders again, I suppose?"

Aldyth's smile vanished. "How did you hear?"

"Cousin Henry told me a fortnight ago."

"Oh, heavens, is he poking his nose into my business?" Lady Aldyth asked, showing a spark of temper. "I wish he would not. He only puts you into a worry. Besides, I've told him time and again that I would not hang on his sleeve, and I haven't."

"Nonetheless we are connections of his."

"That is something we cannot be blamed for," her mother said firmly. "And the next time I see Henry I shall tell him not to poke his nose into my affairs."

"Have you been to the moneylenders again?" Davida asked, determined to know the worst.

"Well, of course I have," Lady Aldyth said sunnily. "Messrs. Smith and King, quite pleasant gentlemen, not the type of beasts I was afraid they might be," she confided.

"They fully understand the problems of a lady in my position and were able to part with the sums quite willingly."

Davida was not entirely convinced by this pleasant portrait of the moneylenders, who had the reputation of being a hardened breed.

"Mama, you must promise me you won't apply to them again."

"Davida!"

"Promise me, please."

"Very well, I promise. I think they have extended me as much credit as they were going to, anyway," she conceded.

Having won this promise from her parent, Davida toyed with the idea of asking for a second, namely, that Lady Aldyth refrain from cards hereafter. But that, she supposed, would be futile. The only solution was to marry her off, and quickly!

CHAPTER EIGHT

HARD ON THE HEELS of the Coopers' appearance at Almack's came invitations to rout parties, balls, and musicales. Although it was late in the Season, not everyone had deserted the city, and the hostesses who remained felt the advantage of having the newcomers at their soirées.

Dutifully, Davida assumed the mantle of a young lady out to land a husband, attending on successive nights Lady Cunningham's rout party, Lady Fortescue's ball, and Mrs. Peabody's musicale. She had scarcely time to catch her breath before she was whisked off to Drury Lane, and finally finished her week at the opera.

For the second time since her arrival in London, she was Lyall's guest at the opera, and while her first visit had not occasioned comment in the press, her second did.

"Do listen to this," Cassie said to Davida on Saturday morning as they breakfasted together. She had the pages of the *Morning Post* spread out on the Pembroke table.

"'At the theatre and seen taking in supper together were the Earl of Exley and Lady Aldyth Cooper. Exley's son, Lord Lyall, and Miss Davida Cooper were also present. Now who is chaperoning whom? The wags at White's say Exley has the advantage over Lyall in the hunt for the lovely Coopers.'"

"Good heavens, let me see that!" Davida snatched the paper from her sister's hands. "What an awful gossip! I dearly hope Mama doesn't see it. Or Lyall! He'll be livid."

"See what?" asked that gentleman's sister as she breezed into the room.

"See this," Cassie said, waving the column.

Lady Susan, who was too vain to wear the reading glasses she needed, held the paper out at arm's length. "Lord Stanley to wed Lady Sherwood? Good gracious, I can scarcely credit it," she exclaimed, riveted by this item. "Do you remember her? No, I don't think you have met her. She is abominably fat with three chins. Stanley has been wearing the willow for her for years, ever since she was a girl and preferred Sherwood to him, or so the story goes. And Sherwood has been dead these ten years, so it seems that he has won her. Such devotion! I thought it mere flourishing on his part, but the *tendre* must be strong to have weathered three chins. Two I could see—"

"Lady Susan, not that. That!" Cassie said, pointing out the item about Lyall and Exley.

"I have half a mind to march down to that newspaper and tell that writer a thing or two." Davida rose, fuming.

"Oh, heavens, don't do that!" Susan exclaimed immediately. "This item is not so very bad."

Davida paced. "It's bound to infuriate Lyall."

"Oh, I'm sure of it," Susan said cheerfully.

Something in Susan's face brought Davida up short. "Susan, you are not in the least dismayed by this, are you?"

"No."

"Did you have anything to do with it?" Davida asked.

"I told the writer about you and your mother going to the opera with Lyall and Papa," Lady Susan said, handing the paper back to Cassie.

"Told her! Why?" Davida asked, thunderstruck.

"A little prodding can never hurt, my dear. Especially when it comes to as intractable a pair as Papa and Lyall."

"My thoughts exactly!" Cassie agreed before Davida could say a word. She had been obliged to witness Hugh's daily visits to Upper Wimpole Street, and would have prodded Lyall herself if she had known how.

"We can't have Hugh steal a march on Lyall."

"Cassie is right," Susan said as Davida directed a quelling look at her sister. "Hugh has been most attentive to you. You stood up with him twice at Lady Cunningham's party."

Davida sank down on a chair. "What else could I do?" she protested. "Hugh seems always underfoot."

"Yes. Large gentlemen do have that disadvantage," Susan agreed. "I hope you are not too annoyed with me for the item. I really didn't mean to vex you, and I didn't really intend to see you and Lyall teased in print, as much as my father and your mother."

"Your father and my mother," Davida repeated, looking bewildered. "But why? Good heavens, Susan, are you serious?"

Lady Susan threw back her head and laughed. "I wondered that you did not realize earlier what we were up to. It has been in the works for some time now. Papa is so intractable, however, that Jeremy and I together seem obliged to light a fire under him."

"But the earl isn't in love with Mama. I can see that plainly."

"One needn't be in love to marry, particularly at their age. But they would make a comfortable pair. That's what I thought at the beginning, and Lyall agreed."

"Lyall agreed? Do you mean he knows about this scheme?"

"He knows, and he is even more anxious to have your mother as our stepmother than I am!"

These lighthearted words did not spark any levity in Davida's own breast. Obviously, the mere notion of marriage to her was so repugnant that Lyall was prepared to sacrifice his own father on the altar of matrimony.

"I don't know if I like the idea of coercing your father into marrying Mama."

"Oh, it shan't be coercion," Susan said. "And really every gentleman needs to be coerced. Even my own Walter fought shy of making the offer. I nearly had to do it for him," she confessed with a laugh.

"Didn't you think that story Susan told us was the most romantic you've ever heard?" Cassie asked after Lady Susan had departed.

"No, I do not. Their scheme is the outside of enough!"

"I don't mean about their father and our mother. I mean about Lord Stanley finally winning Lady Sherwood. Waiting all these years for her so patiently. Perhaps there is a gentleman in Mama's past who may come forward to claim her!"

SUCH A ROMANTIC SCENARIO was not to be realized, for the only man who came forward out of Lady Aldyth's past was Mr. Brakeworth. On Monday morning he arrived to find the chairs in the sitting room occupied by Sir Edwin Jeffries, Lyall, the ever-present Hugh Sylvester, General Summerfield, who had made Aldyth's acquaintance at the musicale, and the Marquis of Alwyn, who had met Aldyth at the opera with Exley—a fact that the gossip columnist had failed to include in her column.

The sight of these notables afflicted Mr. Brakeworth in the worst possible way. In all his years in London he had never so much as exchanged nods with Lyall or the general, and now to see these gentlemen lavishing attention on his cousins! Mr. Brakeworth did not even try to prevent the envy from showing on his face.

"You have been quite busy in London these past days," he said to Aldyth as she passed him a plate of biscuits.

"Oh, yes. Everyone has been so kind. We've been to the opera and Drury Lane. So many parties. It's a wonder that I am not fagged to death."

"Indeed. I could not credit some of the stories I had been hearing. One might take you for a hurly-burly sort, my dear."

"Hurly-burly!" Aldyth looked taken aback by such a remark.

"Yes," Mr. Brakeworth went on, realizing that he had the attention of everyone in the room. "As your relation I would feel it necessary to point out the folly of allowing yourself or your reputation to be fuel for the prattle boxes."

"If you mean those items in the gossip columns," Aldyth said coldly, "they were none of my doing."

"One ought to refrain from appearing in print."

"You might as well say that one ought to refrain from going anywhere in society. It is one of the penalties one has to pay for living in London," Lyall said quietly. "The gossips make it a habit of bandying one's name in print. No doubt you have discovered that yourself, Mr. Brakeworth."

Mr. Brakeworth flushed under this gentle rebuke, for everyone in the room knew full well he had never attended the functions that might give rise to speculation in the gossip columns.

"There is one thing I do know," Mr. Brakeworth said coldly, "and that is how to pay off my gaming debts." He flashed a malevolent smile at Aldyth, who flushed at his words.

"Do you?" the marquis said affably. "Quite a splendid accomplishment, I'm sure. Would you care to play a hand of whist sometime at White's?"

"I am not a member of White's," Mr. Brakeworth said curtly. He rose. "And I will not suffer to be made a target of fun in my own cousin's sitting room." He departed, angrily jabbing his Malacca cane into the rug.

"Oh, dear, now Henry is angry," Aldyth said with a sigh.

"I thought you were exaggerating your cousin's faults the day we met," Lyall said to Cassie, "but I think you were too charitable by half. Is he really a relation?"

"Unfortunately, yes," Davida said. "Though I don't know why he would come to pinch and scold us, for he had as good as washed his hands of us."

"Reminds me of a fellow on Wellington's staff," Hugh said. "A veritable bag pudding, even Wellington thought as much."

Alwyn strolled over to Lady Aldyth's side. "I beg your pardon, if I caused your cousin any embarrassment. I didn't mean to make him a target of fun."

"Oh, no," Aldyth protested. "I know that. It's just that Henry is just Henry. So starched up when he has nothing to be starched up about. And I am grateful to you for coming to my defence."

"Always happy to oblige a lady in distress," Alwyn said with a smile.

Hugh, having concluded his story about Wellington, discovered that Davida was bidding Sir Edwin goodbye and hastened towards her. As she turned from the doorway, she saw him approach.

"Are you going, Hugh?" she asked.

"Yes, but don't forget about our ride tomorrow."

"I shan't," she said as he disappeared from sight.

"Riding in the park with Hugh **again**, Miss Cooper?" Lyall asked, strolling up to Davida.

"Were you eavesdropping, Lyall?"

"Not at all, but I was about to make my goodbyes when I chanced to hear Hugh making his. Will he be exercising his team in the park?"

She saw no harm in telling him about Hugh's plans. He was taking her to view the abbey ruins to the north, which were said to be quite charming, and then to have a quiet picnic together.

"If one were a spider, I daresay one would find the ruins charming. They are rather dusty and cobwebbed."

"I shall find them charming, I'm sure," Davida said, a warning light in her eyes.

"Just don't wear that white walking dress or you'll regret it," he said, following the marquis out the door after the latter said his farewells.

The next morning Davida toured the ruins of the abbey, a small honey-coloured stone building with a belfry from which a heavy iron bell still hung. She was pleased to see that the ruins were charming.

"An order of monks used to live here," Hugh explained, helping her down from her horse. A huge picnic hamper was hooked onto his saddle. "That was before the other houses arose with their accompanying tide of visitors. Not so bad," he said, grinning, "unless you happen to be a monk. So after a time the monks left for more cloistered quarters."

They explored some of the deserted rooms, which were, Davida was forced to admit to herself, as dusty as Lyall had predicted. She sneezed several times.

"There is a legend about this place," Hugh said, leading her again into the open air of the courtyard. "A pair of lovers on their way to Gretna Green stayed the night here and liked it so much that it is rumoured they never did reach Gretna."

"A pretty tale."

"And utterly false," a voice added as Lyall emerged from behind a pillar.

"Lyall, what are you doing here?" Hugh asked, not pleased to have his private outing with Davida interrupted.

"He was eavesdropping, of course," Davida said cordially.

"I was merely passing by and noticed your horses. I hope I did not interrupt a conspiracy or a rendezvous?"

"Of course we are not having a rendezvous," she said vehemently, too vehemently to suit Hugh. "And what do you mean by calling the tale of the lovers false?"

"They were a pair of bran-faced brats, refused permission to marry for good reason. They were both too young. And as for a night in the abbey, I personally can think of no gloomier place in Christendom to spend a night, if I were on the run to Gretna, quite probably with a bride who would indulge in a fit of vapours at the very idea of putting up here!"

"If you were on the run to Gretna, vapours would be the least of any woman's troubles," Davida retorted. "And you have spoiled a romantic tale. I'd liefer have lovers young and beautiful than spoiled and bran-faced."

"That's Lyall for you. He hasn't an ounce of romance."

"And you do, I suppose?" Lyall asked, pinching off a piece of cobweb that had attached itself to Hugh's jacket. "I could tell Miss Cooper some unromantic tales about you."

"I shouldn't wish to hear them," Davida said promptly. "And if I did I'd apply to Lady Susan. She knows more about you two than anyone else."

"Yes, she does," Lyall agreed with a wary look at Hugh.

"I wonder if we have time for a look at the rest of the abbey before our picnic," Davida said to Hugh.

"By all means," Hugh assured her, "but I'm certain that Jeremy has more important things to do than bother with an old abbey."

To which Lyall, looking amused, replied that there was none that he could think of at the moment. He followed Davida into the building.

CHAPTER NINE

WHILE LYALL TASKED the patience of Hugh and Davida, his parent was doing much the same with the beleaguered Lord Timothy Fife. Using Alwyn's interest in the stables as an excuse, the earl had accompanied the marquis to Fife's estate, where he renewed his attempt to win the bay.

"Good Jove, Exley, the answer is no!" Lord Timothy exclaimed. "Take another of my cattle, but the bay is promised to my daughter. I've told you that."

"She won't know the difference!"

"You don't know Katie," Timothy averred. "Only fifteen and nearly as horse mad as you; she'll notice the switch."

"The grey is more than tolerable," Alwyn interjected, trying to persuade his friend to let drop the matter of the bay.

The earl, however, was not interested in the grey. "I've got a pair of greys. It's the bay I want." He marched off across the lawn.

The marquis exchanged a sympathetic look with Lord Timothy. "George is a bit out of sorts these days."

"So I see. Is it true he's about to take a leg shackle?"

"Hush!" Alwyn said. "Don't let him hear that. He nearly had an attack of apoplexy when he read the item in the *Morning Post*. Tell me about your Arabians."

Lord Timothy fell in willingly with this change of topic, and by the end of the hour Alwyn believed that he had found the bloodstock he wanted.

"How long are you in London?" Timothy asked.

"Perhaps another week."

"I'll have my man of business draw up the documents," he assured Alwyn as they went back into his house, where they found Exley trying to cajole Katie out of her love of the bay.

"Haven't you noticed that sore fetlock it has?" the earl entreated.

"Sore fetlock?" Katie, freckled and smudged with dirt, hooted. "Papa, your friend doesn't have an eye for horses at all."

The earl rose with what dignity he had remaining and he and Alwyn made their farewell.

"Cheer up, George," Alwyn said as they returned to London. "You can't blame him for keeping his promise to his daughter."

"I know. At least you found the cattle you were after. I suppose you will be returning to Ireland?"

"In another week or fortnight, I suppose. If you've tired of my company I can always return to the Connaught."

"I don't mean that!" the earl expostulated. "Pleased to have you. Need to have some company. Can't even set foot in White's without some fool grinning at me and talking fustian rubbish about Lady Aldyth."

"Yes, and that reminds me, Lady Susan came by to make sure we hadn't forgotten about Vauxhall this evening with her and her family."

"Oh botheration!" Exley exploded. "I'd wager a monkey that the Coopers will be there."

The marquis did not take the earl up on this wager, which was a very good thing, for the Coopers were in attendance that evening. The earl, although a civil gentleman, had all he could do to return Lady Aldyth's pleasant greeting, and he left the burden of conversation to Alwyn, who managed to step into the breach very nicely.

"I don't think your father is very happy with my mother," Davida said to Lyall as they walked along the pathway, following the others.

For this evening's outing she wore a gown of sapphire blue, which she had trimmed and refurbished herself.

"You don't know my father. I assure you he is cast into transports."

She laughed. "Oh, what an outrageous whisker. Poor Lord Exley looks as though Mama were going to eat him."

"Yes, and speaking of eating, did you ever taste anything worse than those chicken legs Hugh had in his picnic hamper?"

"I found nothing amiss in the chicken."

"He must have given you the good pieces," Lyall said fretfully. "I nearly broke a tooth!"

"If you had, it would have been your fault. You could see plainly that he did not want you on the picnic."

"Yes, poor Hugh. Although perhaps I shouldn't call him poor, lest you think him destitute. He has a very good income from those estates in Kent. I daresay he has told you about them?"

"Yes," she said. Hugh had spoken in exhaustive detail about his properties, inviting her and her family to visit him any time.

"And he is also his uncle's heir."

Davida turned round. The moonlight was full on her face. "Why are you telling me all this about Hugh? You sound as though I were on the catch for a fortune, when all I want..."

"Is a position as a governess. Or have you thought better of that addled plan?"

She shrugged a shoulder. "It's not addled."

"If your choice is between becoming a governess and becoming Mrs. Hugh Sylvester, I'd take Hugh."

"Your opinions are of no interest, my lord. And in the future I hope you will refrain from intruding on me and Hugh."

"As you wish. I just thought you might need a chaperon on your picnic today."

She choked. "Chaperon!"

"Yes, otherwise the next item in the gossip column of the *Gazette* might be about you and Hugh!"

"They wouldn't dare!"

"I'd advise you to conduct your flirtation with Hugh with more discretion!"

"We aren't flirting! And why am I explaining myself to you? My friendship with Hugh is none of your affair."

"On the contrary, I have a good deal of interest in it. For once you wed Hugh or anyone else I daresay that marriage contract would not be enforceable!"

"Not if Cassie wants to take you!"

He laughed. "I rely on the good Captain Fitzwilliam to save me from that."

"And from that look on your father's face it is apparent that he wishes someone would save him from Parson's Mousetrap. Really, Lyall, how could you plot such a thing?"

"It was Susan who hatched the plot," he protested.

"But you have assisted her."

"I'd sooner stop a flood than Susan when she has a maggot on her brain," he said, as they paused to watch the fireworks lighting up the sky. "Not to worry," he reassured her. "For if Papa does marry your mama, that would make us, well, brother and sister!"

The idea of being a sister to Lyall was one that disturbed Davida, but if Exley did marry Lady Aldyth that was what she would be. How curious to have him for a brother, she thought later that evening as she went to bed. Lyall, a brother. What an addled idea that was!

THE NEXT MORNING Lyall was roused from his bed with the news that Exley was belowstairs. Remembering only too well the last visit of his father to his residence, Lyall hastened into the drawing room to find the earl pacing furiously back and forth.

"Papa, never tell me that you have unearthed another marriage contract for me," he implored.

The earl halted. "Hah! You were right, Lyall. I should have shown Miss Cooper the door, despite her being Cutter's daughter."

"It's a bit late in the day for that," Lyall pointed out.

His father puffed out his cheeks in despair. "It's a bit late for me, as well. I don't know how the devil the prattle boxes get wind of things, but will you look at this?" He handed his son the latest copy of the *Morning Post*.

"'Seen at Vauxhall last evening were the Earl of Exley and Lady Aldyth Cooper, enjoying a solitary stroll down the pathways.'" Lyall read aloud. "Papa, did you stroll with Lady Aldyth?"

"No. That is . . . Well, yes, after a fact. She wanted a better view of the fireworks and so I helped her stand down and escorted her. I couldn't leave her alone in the dark." He sank into the Hepplewhite chair.

"No, you certainly could not," Lyall agreed. "Well, Papa, what are you going to do?"

Exley threw his arms ceilingward. "What I must do! What it seems everyone has predicted I will do. I must marry the dratted female."

"Lady Aldyth?"

"Whom else have I compromised?"

"Did you compromise her?"

"No," his father snorted. "But try and tell the quizzes that."

"Well, Papa, perhaps it shan't be so bad! Lady Aldyth is most congenial," he said heartily, encouraging his parent to look at the brighter side of things.

"I know. It's just that I hadn't anticipated marrying ever again. I dearly loved your mama, Lyall, and I have missed her. But all the same, I go on very comfortably by myself. It will be a change to have a female under my roof. Getting in my way, if you know what I mean?"

"Of course, Papa. You may rely on me to do everything I can to help you!" Lyall said, unable to suppress a twinge of guilt at the sight of his father's face.

The earl rose now with ponderous dignity. "I'd best get it over with. I thought perhaps, if you had no pressing business this morning, you might come with me?"

Seeing that his father was in need of support, Lyall did not hesitate in cancelling his morning round at Jackson's Saloon. But by the time they reached Upper Wimpole Street, Exley's agitated mood had turned to gloom.

John, the butler, looked surprised to see them. "Lady Aldyth is still abovestairs, my lord. I shall fetch her," he said, ushering them into the parlour, where Davida found them minutes later.

She herself had just finished dressing when John sent word of the early-morning callers.

"Would you care to join me for breakfast?" she asked. "Or perhaps just some coffee?"

"No coffee, but do you have any Madeira?" Lord Exley asked.

Davida did not know what to make of this request, which hinted of dire habits indeed in Lyall's family.

"Perhaps just a sherry," Lyall interposed.

The earl disposed of his glass of sherry with one toss. His son prudently refrained from pouring another for him. It would never do to have the earl foxed when he offered for Lady Aldyth.

"That was an excellent show last night at Vauxhall," Lyall said.

"That's what you think," Exley barked. Then, "Ah, Lady Aldyth." He greeted Davida's mother with relief.

"Good morning, Lyall, Lord Exley," Lady Aldyth said, looking as though she were in the habit of rising at nine in the morning. She looked so youthful that Lyall felt better about his father's impending marriage.

"My father is desirous of speech with you, Lady Aldyth," Lyall said. "Miss Cooper, I wonder if you might lend me that book of Byron you bought the other day," he added with a meaningful look at Davida.

Davida was no slow top and she followed this lead smoothly, exiting with Lyall. But as soon as they were out of the parlour she demanded to know what was afoot.

"It's obvious. Papa is preparing to put his fate to the touch."

"Really! Good heavens! Where's Cassie? I shall have to let her know."

She found her sister still asleep and all attempts to rouse her were futile.

"I decided to let her sleep," Davida announced, returning to the sitting room where Lyall was waiting, "since nothing makes me so ill-tempered as to be awakened prematurely, and that goes for most people. But I brought the Byron for you, in case you really did wish to see it."

"Thank you," he said, taking the book.

She peered at the closed doors. "Are they still in there?"

"Yes," Lyall said. "It's been nearly ten minutes, but Papa being Papa it may take a full hour before he gets to the point of his visit."

In actual fact the earl was rapidly reaching his Rubicon.

"Lady Aldyth," he said, interrupting her remarks about the Fogarty musicale and the abominable harp playing of Miss Fogarty. "I must say something to you."

"Yes, of course, Lord Exley," Aldyth agreed, looking up expectantly at him.

The sight of that face nearly caused the earl to bolt, but he swallowed hard and took his fences in a rush. "I think it best if... well, I mean, all things considered... I know the prattle boxes have been talking of nothing else to me.... Well, dash it all, don't you think it best if you married me?"

Lady Aldyth stared at him, stunned by his words. "Lord Exley, are you making me an offer?" she demanded.

"Yes, of course!" He scowled.

"Well, I am obliged to you. It is very civil of you and quite an honour, but I can't possibly—"

"Can't possibly?" The black frown vanished from Exley's brow. "Do you mean... My good Lady Aldyth, are you refusing me?" he exclaimed joyfully.

"I hope you are not too dashed down," Lady Aldyth said quickly.

"Dashed down, oh, no. Well...just a trifle," Exley said, wiping his forehead. "I mean, more than a trifle. What a turnabout this is! Even Lyall was as good as saying what an excellent stepmother you would make."

"Really?" Lady Aldyth asked. "I had rather seen myself in the role of his mother-in-law."

Exley knitted his brow. "Oh, sits the wind in that corner?"

"I hope it will before our time in London is up." She rose. "And now, my lord, do you think you would like some breakfast? It is very early."

"Yes, I do think my appetite is back," Exley agreed, and they went out of the parlour arm in arm.

CHAPTER TEN

AT THE SIGHT of the beaming faces on the two exiting the parlour, Davida felt her heart sink within her breast. But that was idiotish, she told herself at once; she wanted her mother married and settled. And Lord Exley, by everything she had been told, was a kind and generous man who would undoubtedly cosset her mother outrageously.

Perhaps it was just the idea of being forever tied to Lyall as sister to brother that was making her feel out of sorts, she decided, as Lyall took advantage of her wool-gathering to wish his father and her mother happy.

"Happy? Yes, I am deuced happy," his father agreed. "Devil take it, lad, Aldyth has more sense than any woman I ever knew."

"You are too kind, Exley." Lady Aldyth laughed. "Oh, Davida, dear, I have invited Exley to stay for breakfast. You must too, Lyall. Will you tell John, dear?"

"Of course, Mama," Davida said immediately. "I will ask him if there is any champagne to celebrate your coming marriage."

These words were greeted with a trill of laughter from her mother and a guffaw from the earl.

Her mother recovered first. "Do give over the champagne. I vow if I drink any at this hour I shall have a headache."

"Papa," Lyall said abruptly, staring from face to face, "did you offer for Lady Aldyth or not?"

"Oh, I offered, right enough, my boy." Exley grinned. "And she refused me."

"Refused!" On her way out to fetch John, Davida halted in her tracks. "Mama, you didn't!"

"Yes, of course I did, Davida," Lady Aldyth said. "Not that it wasn't an honour, which it is, but Exley no more wishes to marry me than I he. It is just those ridiculous gossips."

"Yes, and if I ever find out who has been informing that columnist about my activities, I shall strangle him!" Exley threatened.

Lyall exchanged glances with Davida.

"Oh, there is no necessity to do that," Aldyth protested.

"To do what?" Cassie asked. She had come down the stairs and, having just left her bed, was blinking at the sight of their guests.

"Cassie, my love, you are just in time for breakfast. Do let me tell you everything that has transpired while you have been sleeping," her mother offered.

As Lady Aldyth took Cassie and Exley into the dining room, Davida drew Lyall aside. "So much for your great plan, my lord."

"Even great plans come to grief, as Napoleon himself might have told you."

"You are beginning to sound like Hugh," Davida said tartly. "I wish never to hear another word about Napoleon or Wellington. What are we to do now about Mama?"

"What can we do?" he retorted. "You certainly cannot blame me for your mother's actions."

"No, but it was an idiotish notion in the first place to think of Lord Exley and Mama together. You should have found her someone more suitable."

He recoiled as if stung. "My father is eminently suitable. If you remember your strictures to me, you wanted someone kind, and generous, and willing to marry her. Well, he fit that description, and she refused. Perhaps your mama does not wish to be married, Miss Cooper. Have you thought of that?''

Davida would not own to any such thing, but later, after breakfast when she was alone with her mother, she began to delve into the reasons behind Lady Aldyth's refusal of Exley.

''Mama, did you refuse the earl because of Papa?''

''Papa?'' Aldyth looked up, momentarily confused. ''Oh, you think I am still mourning your father, do you, Davida?''

''Exley is a good catch, if you forgive my vulgar speech!''

''Yes, I know. And for a moment there, I was tempted. It would improve our circumstances, that goes without question. But I couldn't. Sheer terror was on his face.''

''Then you might have married him if he weren't so terrified of the idea? It wasn't just Papa?''

Lady Aldyth turned, an enigmatic expression in her eyes. ''I daresay it was, and it wasn't. Oh, pray, don't tease me about it, Davida. I'm sure that any other widow in my circumstances would have snatched him up. But I knew well enough he was being coerced into it by those items in the columns. And I suppose I am being as romantic as Cassie when I say that if I did marry again, I'd like it to be for love.'' She paused, a faraway look in her eyes, then shook her head abruptly. ''Now, that is enough romantic bibble-babble. I vow I am beginning to sound like Cassie. Since I am up so early, do you think you would like to accompany me to Fanchon's? I have ordered some new dresses.''

Davida fell in readily enough with this suggestion, but later at Fanchon's shop she almost wished she hadn't accompanied her mother, for the modiste insisted on some payment of her delinquent bills before she allowed Lady Aldyth to take the new dresses.

"But this is outrageous," Lady Aldyth protested. "If you did not wish our business why did you take our order?"

"You had assured me that the monies would be arriving," Fanchon said. "I do not like to do this, *madame*, but I am just a poor working woman."

At this outrageous whisker Davida blinked. Fanchon dressed the leading ladies of society and by no measure could be considered poor. Added to that, her staff of girls did the bulk of the stitchery.

"You will have your money by this afternoon," Aldyth said, sweeping grandly out of the shop, followed by Davida.

"Mama, what are you going to do? You are not going to the moneylenders, are you?"

"No, of course not!" Aldyth said dismissively, putting on her gloves. "I promised you I would not, and I always keep my promises. I am tempted just to let Fanchon hang on to her odious dresses! But I cannot, since if word of that got round, well..." She shrugged. "No, I will do what I should have done long ago."

"Which is?" Davida demanded.

"I shall sell my jewels."

"Your jewels? Mama, you can't!"

"Well, of course I can!" Lady Aldyth replied. "I sold several pieces right after Papa died to get us through some of the worse times. Now I'll sell the rest."

"If you are selling yours, you must take my sapphires as well."

"No, Davida," Lady Aldyth protested. "They were the one thing your aunt left you. I shall never touch them. Now, let me just think. I have the emeralds and the rubies. That should be enough to pay off Fanchon."

"Whom will you sell the jewels to?"

"To someone who has long admired them. And actually, it will be a way of keeping them in the family."

"In the family?"

"Yes. I'll sell them to Cousin Henry!"

"Mama, no!"

"Yes, he has always envied me the jewels. And he'll be so pleased that I have been reduced to selling them to him!" Lady Aldyth predicted with a remarkable reading of Mr. Brakeworth's character.

She returned to Upper Wimpole Street for the jewels, and then it was on to Mr. Brakeworth's. That gentleman was at first aggrieved to find his cousin calling on him, but he could not conceal a twitch of eagerness in his hands as he took the rubies and emeralds from her.

"So, you have been reduced to this, have you, Aldyth?" he asked with what struck Davida as more than his usual lack of tact.

"Yes," Aldyth answered without too much emotion. "So if you will give me a fair price for them, Henry, I would be obliged to you. That is, if you wish to buy them. If not, I can go elsewhere."

"Oh, I'll buy them," Henry agreed. "But of course you know the setting is very old-fashioned and the jewels themselves show sign of use."

"The jewels themselves are stunning!" Davida interjected. She would not stand by to watch her mother cheated.

"Now, now, Davida, Henry won't cheat me," Lady Aldyth said, looking amused, "will you, Henry?"

Mr. Brakeworth stiffened. "I am not a cheat, cousin. I shall give you a fair price for them. A very fair price, indeed."

After ten minutes of dickering, Lady Aldyth accepted Mr. Brakeworth's cheque for the jewels, but Davida, for her part, could not help regretting that circumstances had forced them to make such a sale.

"Oh, don't repine, Davida," Lady Aldyth said cheerfully. "I vow the new dresses will do us more good than

stupid jewels. And I did wish to look my best at Lady Veaseley's ball tomorrow night.''

''You always look charming, Mama.''

''Thank you, dear. But this time I want to look stunning!''

This declaration startled Davida. Lady Veaseley was a
simple soul, not very high in the instep; why should her
mother wish to cut a swath through her ballroom? She
wondered if the reason was all the buzz in the *Morning Post*.
Thinking of the gossip made her wonder if Exley would be
present at Lady Veaseley's ball; his friend, Alwyn, was a
connection of Lady Veaseley's.

THE FOLLOWING EVENING Davida, garbed in an exquisite
gown of the palest primrose sarsenet with her dark hair be-
guilingly piled high in a knot from which a few choice ringlets were allowed to drape at the neck, swept into her
mother's bedchamber to find that good lady absorbed in the
finishing touches of her own toilette.

''Mama,'' she exclaimed raptly, ''you look wonderful!''

Lady Aldyth, who did look particularly radiant that evening in the new emerald-green satin from Fanchon, favoured her elder daughter with a happy smile.

''You don't think it too much?'' she asked anxiously.

Davida shook her head and the ringlets bounced on the
back of her neck. ''Good heavens, no. I shall just see if
Cassie is ready!''

Some of Lady Aldyth's enthusiasm had spilled onto
Davida, who found herself hopeful that her mama might
meet a suitable gentleman, who in turn might be a future
stepfather. She entered Cassie's room, and was stunned to
find her sister still curled up in a dressing gown with her nose
buried in a book.

''You are supposed to be dressing!'' she wailed, snatching up the offending book and scanning with a shudder its

more lurid passages. "Where did you get this from?" she demanded.

"Hugh bought it for me the other day, don't you recall?" Cassie said.

"Well, you shall ruin your eyes if you read in such poor light. Get up and dress, Cassie. It's nearly time for us to go."

Cassie opened her wardrobe, protesting all the while that she didn't wish to be bored by a lot of stuffy gentlemen.

"I hope they shan't be stuffy, too," Davida agreed. "Aren't you enjoying our time in London at all?"

"I would enjoy it more if Bruce were here," Cassie said with a sigh as she struggled with a row of buttons.

"Bruce will be here soon," Davida soothed. "By the by, I hope you have written to him that you have recovered from that bogus attack of scarlet fever!"

Cassie giggled. "Oh, yes, I've told him all about our London doings."

"Good," Davida said, though she wondered why that mischievous look was back in Cassie's eyes.

Lady Veaseley was not one of Society's premier hostesses—indeed, in certain circles she had a reputation as a recluse—but on this evening she was assisted by Lord Alwyn, who was serving as host; Lord Veaseley was in Brighton playing whist with the Duke of York's set.

As Davida entered the ballroom with her mother and sister, she found Hugh at her side.

"You are looking beautiful tonight, Miss Cooper," he said, with such obvious appreciation that Cassie, standing nearby, despaired of ever putting an end to that *tendre*.

"You are looking very handsome yourself," Davida retorted. "I know one is not supposed to say such things to gentlemen, which has always struck me as absurd, since gentlemen take as much pains with their dress as do ladies, particularly those wont to follow in Mr. Brummell's footsteps."

"Good evening, Miss Cooper." Lyall had strolled up. "Talking about the Beau to your beau, I see?"

"Good evening, Lyall," Davida returned coldly.

Hugh did not appear to notice the frostiness of her reply. "Where is your father, Jeremy?" he asked. "I would think that after this morning's notice he would make an appearance with Lady Aldyth."

"He did more than that. He made her an offer this morning, which she declined."

"Really!" Hugh was thunderstruck. "Good heavens! I thought it as good as set."

"Yes, so did we."

"I hope you are not as indisposed to the idea of matrimony as your mother," he said to Davida with a meaningful look.

"Lyall, don't you wish to dance with Davida?" Cassie blurted out.

"An excellent suggestion, Miss Cassie," Lyall agreed with aplomb. "Miss Cooper?" he asked. Later, as he was waltzing her about the ballroom, he explained that he was sure she did not really wish to receive Hugh's offer in a ballroom. Or did she?

"An offer from Hugh? That's preposterous."

He clucked his tongue at her. "My dear Miss Cooper, he had all the look of a man about to put his fate to the touch. You forget I saw just that same look on my father's face yesterday morning. I know such things."

"And I know you are roasting me. I don't see why you are so interested in my affairs."

"Sheer self-defence," he said, expertly waltzing her down the length of the room, causing the ringlets to bounce against her neck. "It is through your actions, I remind you, that I have taken an interest in your family's affairs. I was blissfully going my own way," he continued, not heeding her attempt to speak, "embroiled in nothing more tedious

than my own daily life until you saw fit to bring our paths
to cross."

"That was because of the contract," she reminded him.
"And knowing my own papa's soundness of mind and with
all due respect to Lord Exley, I can't help thinking it was
your relation who dreamed up this skip-brained idea in the
first place!"

Lyall manfully conceded that the earl might have been in
some measure responsible for their present predicament.
"Of course he could not have foreseen back then how irri-
tating it would be for us to be saddled with each other."

"Quite true, and irritation is much too small a word for
what I feel. But since the music is at an end, I think we
needn't be saddled with each other a second longer, and I
assure you, my lord, once we leave London, I shan't embroil you in any more of my stupid affairs."

His reaction to these words was so sceptical that Davida
nearly succumbed to an urge to box his ears. She stalked
away before she gave in to the impulse, almost colliding with
Lady Susan and the Honourable Walter Thackerly.

"Good heavens, Davida, you look all atwitter."

"I've just had a horrid quarrel with Lyall."

"I wouldn't have thought Jeremy had the wit to be quarrelsome, my dear," Susan said, laughing. "You must realize by now that he is the complete dunce where ladies are
concerned."

Davida gave her a wry grin. "It's just that he considers me
managing and forward and overbearing, and," she reflected ruefully, snapping her ivory fan shut, "he could be
right. Which makes it all the worse."

"Of course it does," Lady Susan agreed. "And so rag-
mannered of him to point this out to you in the course of
just one waltz!"

Davida was fated to hear more from Lyall, for she found
he was seated next to her at the supper table. She nonethe-

less turned her attention to Viscount Bowlin on her right, as well as to the dinner, which included oysters, a fillet of veal, two dressed ducklings and an abundance of lobster patties. Davida enjoyed every morsel of the food. Perhaps, she admitted to herself with a pang of conscience, she enjoyed them too much, for she was fully conscious that fashion dictated ladies should be skin and bone.

Aside from a few pointed remarks about Davida's capacity for lobster patties, which appeared to rival Cassie's affinity for strawberry tarts, Lyall devoted himself to Lady Fortescue on his left, and Davida spent most of the hour conversing with the viscount on his favourite topic, his health.

As any of Bowlin's friends might attest, he was good for several hours on the history of the various ailments he had suffered from boyhood on and the cures attempted for each.

This flow was finally stemmed by a question from Lady Susan, who sat on the viscount's right, concerning the medicinal properties of a certain herb. As he turned to expound fully to her on that topic, Davida, whose appetite had not unnaturally deserted her during the recitation of the viscount's numerous ills and cures, was once again able to devote herself to the enjoyment of her plate.

CHAPTER ELEVEN

GREAT WAS DAVIDA'S SENSE of pride when she saw the marquis leading her mother out for the first dance after supper. Not so happy was the emotion that beset her when she saw Hugh making his way determinedly toward her. She searched frantically for rescue, intercepting Lyall's ironic gaze, but she would have died before asking him to help her and was forced to acquiesce to the quadrille with Hugh.

"Do you know I have been trying all evening to get a moment to speak to you," he complained.

"Oh, have you? That is what happens at balls, I suppose," she said. "One can scarcely hear oneself think much less talk to anyone at length. I don't think I can take seriously anything anyone says to me in a ballroom, do you?" she went on, well aware that she was babbling like a shatterbrain.

"And why not?" he asked, puzzled.

"Oh, it is the atmosphere of a ball—the lights and the music. I daresay that there has been many a word spoken at a ball that the speaker would wish to have back the next morning."

"Well, I suppose." Hugh frowned. "Perhaps I should speak to you tomorrow at Upper Wimpole Street. We can have a few moments in private."

"That is kind of you, Hugh, but I believe that I am promised to Cassie tomorrow morning. She is desirous of attending a fair outside of London. There will be acrobats and jugglers there."

"I will go with you," Hugh offered, "if you don't mind."

"No, of course not," she said with aplomb, "if Cassie agrees."

Cassie, when the question was put to her, was not too pleased at the prospect of Hugh dangling after Davida, but she gave her reluctant agreement.

"And you must come with us to the fair," she told Lyall a few minutes later when she found him standing with Lady Susan.

"My dear girl, you have gone daft. I haven't been to a fair in ages," Lyall protested.

"Then think of what a splendid entertainment this will be," she continued.

"Have you taken to planning my entertainments?" Lyall demanded with a sigh. "Oh, very well, I give in. I must own that I wonder what I did for amusement before I met you Coopers."

"Well, we can't have Hugh offering for Davida," Cassie pointed out. "And if you don't come along for support, he will do just that."

"How will it sit if I come along too?" Lady Susan asked.

"Oh, famous!" Cassie said. "If you don't think you will be bored, ma'am."

"You weren't afraid that I would be bored!" Lyall protested.

"You're different."

"Indeed he is," Lady Susan agreed. "No, I shan't be bored, my dear. And I heartily concur with you. We can't have Hugh offering for Davida, now can we?" The two ladies exchanged looks of comprehension.

So it was that the following day Davida found herself with a contingent of companions, including both Hugh and Lyall, as she strolled the fairgrounds. She and her sister, both sporting matching wide-brimmed hats, popped in and out of the tents when not watching jugglers balancing balls and acrobats walking on their hands.

Lord Alwyn and Lady Aldyth fell back from the group, appearing more interested in each other than in the entertainments the fair offered. Susan, for her part, discovered an old friend, Lady Foxborough, amid some other theatrical acquaintances and went off with them.

Among the various entertainments for the gentlemen—for it was thought no gently bred female would wish to view such spectacles—were a cockfight and a boxing exhibition. Cassie expressed great interest in the latter, but on this point Davida was adamant. "You are not viewing any horrid boxing mill," she said, taking her sister by the sleeve and leading her away.

To Davida's surprise Lyall came to her aid, informing Cassie that mills were not for young ladies like her.

"Oh no?" Cassie pouted. "They are, I suppose, just for very old gentlemen like you and Hugh?"

Lyall, manfully meeting Hugh's eyes, forbore comment on this point, asking how it would sit if two decrepit gentlemen bought her some ices. Cassie succumbed to the temptation of the ices, and munching these treats, the four strolled about the grounds with Hugh pointing out the various sights to Davida.

After finishing her ice, Cassie caught sight of a nearby gypsy tent and coaxed for permission to have her palm read.

"By all means," Lyall responded. "And you, Miss Cooper?" He turned to Davida.

"No, thank you," Davida answered, "but you go ahead, Cassie." And she added in an undertone, "Do try and behave."

"Don't you wish to know what your future will hold?" Hugh asked as Lyall and Cassie departed.

Davida shook her head. "The whole point of a future is that it's unexpected. Besides," she confessed, laughing, "it is always the same fortune foretold—I shall meet a dark, handsome stranger and he will take me halfway around the world with him.''

Hugh, looking intrigued, inquired if the gentleman who would perform these feats must always be dark.

''Oh, no. That depends entirely on the gypsy's own imagination. Some have told me he would have copper hair, while others prophesied blond.''

''Then there's hope for me,'' Hugh said softly, looking down at her so intently that she was obliged to devour the remains of her ice and send him off for another. A flirtation with Hugh was not what she wanted at all, and yet she was not too displeased by his attentions. From all Lady Susan had told her, Hugh was quite a catch. But I am not on the scramble for a husband, she reminded herself as he reappeared, carrying another ice.

She was still munching on this when Cassie emerged from the gypsy tent, her face aglow. She skipped up to her sister as Lyall trailed behind. ''The gypsy saw Bruce in my future!'' she announced.

''She actually told you his name?'' Davida asked.

''Well, no,'' Cassie admitted. ''But someone dark and far away, and that must be Bruce for who else could it be? She says he is coming back to me very soon.''

''A very satisfactory type of fortune,'' Davida agreed. She turned a quizzing eye toward Lyall, asking if he, too, was satisfied with his fortune.

''Quite satisfied,'' Lyall said promptly.

''Don't keep us on tenterhooks, Jeremy,'' Hugh prompted.

''I am to meet a dazzling beauty, marry her, and carry her around the world,'' Lyall told them, pausing briefly. ''And I do hope that is merely the gypsy's habit of speech, for if I were to carry a lady around the globe—even the lightest one I could find—I should be exhausted after a mile. Unfortunately the gypsy also neglected to mention where I would meet this paragon.''

"Now, that does surprise me," Davida said. "For I would expect that even gypsies would be acquainted with Almack's.''

"But not every beauty is to be found at Almack's, Miss Cooper," Lyall countered, an enigmatic expression flitting across his face.

Lady Aldyth and the marquis drifted up to them just then, and shortly the group was reunited with Lady Susan. Everyone had seen enough at the fair and was ready to return to London. Davida, riding in Hugh's carriage, felt her thoughts drifting as Hugh alternated his usual tales of his hero, Wellington, with such paeans to the Kentish landscape that Davida soon felt a hearty dislike for Kent and its famous cherry orchards.

She was relieved when Hugh set her down at Upper Wimpole Street and wished with all her heart that he would go. But Lady Aldyth, having had a very good day, invited her companions to stay for dinner. Lady Susan was promised elsewhere, but Lyall, Hugh and Lord Alwyn accepted the invitation to dine.

"Don't you wish to go home and change?" Cassie quizzed Hugh.

"Oh, Cassie, there is no need for that!" Lady Aldyth protested. "We are all family here, or near enough to being family," she said with a smile. "It's not a grand dinner, either," she added frankly.

She led the way into the parlour. Davida was about to follow until Hugh took her hand and pulled her into the sitting room.

"Hugh, what are you doing?" she asked as he closed the doors.

"Just trying to have a private word with you," he replied reassuringly. "Rather difficult to do with your mother and everyone else about."

"What do you want to talk about?" she asked.

"Can't you guess?"

"Hugh, please, if this is a riddle, I beg you to try it some other day. My head is truly in a whirl—" Davida broke off as he lifted her chin up with his fingers. Good heavens! she thought.

"Davida, surely you must suspect what I feel for you," Hugh began.

"Hugh, really! You must not!" she protested, regaining custody of her chin temporarily as he possessed himself of the hand nearest him and pressed a fervent if slightly damp salute on its palm.

"Davida, darling. Do you feel for me what I feel for you?"

Davida wanted nothing more than to possess her hand once again and babbled that she wished they would always be friends.

He chuckled. "I want more than friendship, my dear."

"Oh, Hugh, please. I can scarcely think."

"All you need to think about is what a splendid life we shall enjoy as husband and wife."

"Hugh, are you making me an offer of marriage?" Davida asked, amazed.

"Certainly, I'm offering you marriage," he returned, looking so stricken at the possibility of any alternative that a giggle irrepressibly broke loose from her. It ended as soon as he clapped her to his chest.

"We shall have a wonderful life together, Davida, I know it," Hugh promised, trying to plant a kiss on her lips as she struggled to free herself. They were still occupied in this strange tableau when Cassie entered the room, stopping dead upon seeing Davida engaged with Hugh.

"Unhand Davida!" she demanded.

Hugh, conscious of the note of authority in her voice and being by nature an obedient sort of gentleman, obeyed the command. Davida was dropped on the settee to gaze at the tiny Cassie advancing like the wrath of God. This could not be happening!

"Cassie," she pleaded weakly. "Do go away."

"I shall do nothing of the sort," Cassie replied in as grand a manner as Mrs. Siddons. "It's plain Mr. Sylvester has forgotten himself and foisted his very disagreeable attentions on you." Her gaze raked Hugh from head to toe. "You should be ashamed of yourself, sir."

Hugh reddened under this rebuke and stammered out an apology, before recalling that he was being upbraided by a chit little removed from the schoolroom. He then replied with some dignity that he was not foisting his attentions on anyone.

"My sister was fighting you off, sir," Cassie pointed out icily.

"Yes," Davida intervened hastily. "But really, Cassie, he has done nothing so disagreeable. Just perhaps a shade over-eager and nothing to give a repulse. He was making me an offer."

"Of marriage?" Cassie asked sceptically.

Hugh, affronted, as for the second time in mere minutes the purity of his motives was questioned, replied certainly of marriage. "And I must say," he continued in strangled accents, "that I have never offered a lady like yourself anything less than marriage. But why I should be explaining myself to a chit like you, I don't know."

"Well, I couldn't be too certain," Cassie pointed out. "Gentlemen do have their bits of muslin."

"That is enough," Davida erupted, trying to seize control of the situation. "Go away at once."

Cassie balked. "You can't mean to marry him, Davida!"

"And why shouldn't I?" Davida asked impatiently.

"Yes," Hugh echoed, pleased to hear this, "why shouldn't she?"

Cassie, finding herself at a loss to offer any good reason against the match, thrust the burden back on her sister by asking if she were accepting Hugh's offer.

"Yes...no... I'm not certain," Davida stammered, conscious of Hugh looking on. She flung up her hands. "Just do go away, Cassie," she begged. "Having you here at a time like this is not at all the thing."

"Very well." Cassie gave in reluctantly. "But I shall be outside in case you wish any help."

As soon as she had left, Hugh glanced at Davida. "Well, what is it to be? Yes, no, or I'm not certain?"

Davida could not meet his eyes, focusing instead on her hands clasped tightly in her lap. "How can I even begin to make a decision?" she asked. "Not that I am not honoured. But I should like some time to think on my answer."

"But of course," Hugh said.

She smiled gratefully. "In the meantime, do you think we could keep the news of your offer to ourselves?"

"Cassie already knows," he reminded her.

"Yes, but I'll induce her to keep still," Davida told him, knowing that this task was easier said than done.

Cassie, however, who accosted Davida as soon as she left the sitting room demanding to know if she was going to accept Hugh, was surprisingly amenable to Davida's request.

"I haven't said yes or no," Davida explained. "But I want you to keep silent on the matter. You are not to breathe a word of this to anyone. Is that understood?"

"Certainly, certainly," Cassie promised, looking so innocent that Davida rather glumly wondered who would be the first to hear of it.

CHAPTER TWELVE

To Davida's relief Hugh did not press his suit with her during dinner. This did not prevent Lyall, however, from gazing from her to Hugh at the table, as though reading what had passed between them like the pages of an amusing novel.

"Not that he has anything whatsoever to do with my decision," Davida told herself later as they adjourned to the parlour to enjoy a game of jackstraws. They were still in the parlour, with Cassie winning every game, when Davida noticed that the marquis and Aldyth had slipped away to the sitting room.

"Davida, why are you wool-gathering?" Cassie demanded. "It is your turn."

"Oh, is it?" Davida asked, hastily applying herself to the straws.

"Your mind appears to be dwelling on something other than this cheerful game," Lyall observed, taking his turn after her. "I wonder what it could be."

"You may wonder all you like," Davida said, directing a quelling look at both Hugh and Cassie.

"It's Hugh, isn't it?" Lyall said in an offhand way.

Davida stiffened. "I told you before, Lyall, that you would oblige me by not interfering with my personal matters."

"I shouldn't dream of doing any such thing," he drawled. "I was merely pointing out that it was Hugh's turn in the game."

"Oh," she said, looking abashed, and colouring furiously before Lyall's amused eyes.

She was relieved when Cassie won the game, and was wondering how much more of Lyall's company she would be obliged to endure when the door to the sitting room burst open and the marquis came out with Aldyth.

"Oh, my dears," Aldyth exclaimed. "I hate to interrupt your game but if I don't tell you I shall surely burst. Alwyn has made me an offer."

"What?" Davida exclaimed, her irritation with Lyall forgotten.

"Mama, how famous!" Cassie skipped over to hug her mother. "Is it true, sir?"

"It is," Alwyn said with an indulgent smile. "I never thought I would marry, but Aldyth has changed all that. Once I clapped eyes on her, I knew she was the woman for me. Only at the time I thought Exley had the better chance at her. Luckily for me, she turned him down."

"Then you have accepted Alwyn, ma'am?" Lyall asked.

"Oh, yes," Aldyth said, emerging from a tearful embrace with her daughters. Her eyes shone as she gazed at the marquis. "In fact, that was one reason I turned Exley down, because I had begun to . . . well . . . hope that a certain person might be inclined to look my way."

"And he has!" Lord Alwyn laughed.

"Good heavens, this calls for that bottle of champagne," Davida said. "I shall fetch John."

She went out of the parlour and found John in the hall. He looked relieved to see her, because he had just admitted Lord Exley, who was beet-red in the face and muttering something about nursing vipers in his bosom as he strode stiffly along the hall.

"Good evening, Lord Exley," Davida greeted him.

"Ah, Miss Cooper, you would oblige me if you could tell me if Alwyn is present here?"

"Indeed, he is, sir," Davida said. "Will you come this way?"

The earl didn't answer, for he had already stalked into the sitting room, where he took in the happy festivities with a baleful eye. "You!" he accused, pointing a finger at Alwyn. "I should have known. I take you in and what must you do but abuse my hospitality!"

"Exley? Good heavens, what have I done?" Alwyn protested.

The earl walked up to his old friend. "Dissembler! You know very well what you've done. I introduced you, and what must you do but snatch away my heart's desire! It is an insult to my honour," he stated, flinging a glove in the marquis's face.

"Papa, have you gone mad?" Lyall thundered.

"You will name your seconds," Exley demanded.

"No, he will not," Lady Aldyth expostulated. "Exley, I don't know why you are being so intractable."

"If it's a duel you want, a duel you shall have," Alwyn said quietly. "But I saw no harm in taking advantage of the situation."

"Good heavens, Papa!" Lyall pulled his parent away. "Alwyn's right. You yourself made an offer and it came to naught."

"I know, but I was prepared to make a second and a third," Exley said. "Now all that chance is lost to me. When I think of the offspring she could have given me . . ."

At these words Davida started and Lady Aldyth choked.

"Lord Exley, are you speaking of Mama?" Cassie asked incredulously.

"What?" The earl recoiled. "Good Jove, no."

"Then what are you talking about?" the marquis asked in the voice of one driven to the wall.

"Timothy's bay, of course!"

"The bay!" Lyall expostulated.

"Yes, the bay that I have had my heart set on. I went over to visit Timothy today to make another offer, and what must I learn but that you, Alwyn, have bought it!"

"That is why you are angry with the marquis," Davida said, and weak with relief she began to laugh until the tears rolled down her face. Her mother and sister joined her.

"Lyall—" Exley crooked a finger "—I think that you'd best have a doctor in to look at them. I don't think they're queer in the attic yet, but one never knows."

"The only one queer in the attic is you, my friend!" Alwyn said. "And I should take you up on your offer of a duel, but I shan't. That bay, I purchased for you."

"For me?"

"Yes, I knew you had your heart set on it, and I managed to persuade Timothy to sell it to me."

"How the devil did you do that?"

"You weren't at the Veaseley ball, were you?"

The earl shook his head grimly. "I've had my fill of balls."

"Then you didn't see his daughter, Lilian, and Lady Veaseley's second son, all but enamoured of each other. I put it to him that I could help the match along if he wanted me to, which he does, for the lad is a good one. And he was so grateful he agreed to sell me the bay. Which I wanted to give to you."

"Give? Good heavens, Alwyn, that's generous of you."

"I thought it might assuage my guilt at having stolen a march on you with Lady Aldyth."

"Lady Aldyth? Why the devil is everyone talking about Aldyth...? Oh!" He peered more closely into the eyes of his friend. "Good Jove, Alwyn, you offered for Aldyth?"

"That he did," replied Lyall.

The marquis clapped his friend on the shoulder. "And don't be too dashed down when I tell you that she's accepted me!"

The earl, far from being dashed down, was cast in alt when the full reality of his friend's words sank in. His son, too, appeared to be in the best of humour, Davida thought, which was only to be expected in one who had won a reprieve.

Later, while she undressed for bed, Davida brooded on the improbability of there being two offers made in one day: one to her and one to Lady Aldyth. Her mother had had no difficulty in saying yes to the marquis, but what should she tell Hugh? As she brushed her hair, Lady Aldyth knocked on her door.

"Just wanted to say good-night on this best of nights," she explained, coming in.

"Good night, Mama." Davida turned and hugged her. "I am so very happy for you."

"Thank you, dear. I must confess, this has been an exciting day. As Cassie pointed out to me when I told her good-night, I am going to be a marchioness!"

"And I can't think of anyone who will fit that role better than you," Davida said loyally, clasping her mother's hand. "But there is one thing that teases me about your engagement to the marquis, or perhaps you will say it doesn't matter anymore."

"What doesn't matter, child? Are you thinking of my debts? I made a full confession to Alwyn. Indeed, that is what kept us behind doors for so long, for I felt obliged to tell him who my creditors were. And," she added naïvely, "since I have so many of them I had a hard time remembering them all."

Davida laughed. "No, I didn't mean that. Although I am glad that you told Alwyn. He understood?"

"Oh, yes. He is a good man, Davida. So kind."

"Mama, do you recall telling me only days ago that if you did marry again it would be for love?"

"And you wonder if I love Alwyn?" Lady Aldyth inquired. "Well, my dear, I know it must sound ninnyhammerish of me, but yes, I do love him. I liked him the first time I clapped eyes on him, but somehow or another it was always Exley that people were pushing at me. And at my age I couldn't really throw out a lure, but still, Alwyn always did find a way to come over and say a few words to me. And the other night after the Veaseley ball, I was encouraged to hope. And then today at the fair, I just knew he was the one for me. And this evening when he offered for me...!" Lady Aldyth's eyes shone. "I vow my heart raced the way it never did when Exley was offering for me. Do you know what I mean?" she asked Davida, who was smiling at her with a faraway look in her eyes.

"I can imagine, Mama."

Her mother kissed her. "I think we Coopers are just fated to be females who marry for love!"

And where did that leave Hugh? Davida wondered as her mother left her alone.

For most of the night she tossed and turned, eventually falling asleep with the hope that morning would bring some enlightenment. But when the sunlight bathed her room the following day her head felt every bit as muddled as it had the previous night.

Cassie's morning chatter did not augur well for Davida's throbbing temples, and she soon excused herself to stroll in the small Shakespeare garden in back of their house. There Lady Susan found her and invited her on a morning visit to some friends. Feeling somewhat restored by the fresh air, Davida accepted the invitation.

"The Baughs are quite old family friends," Lady Susan explained as they settled themselves into the carriage seat behind the groom. "By the by, I must felicitate you, mustn't I?"

"Felicitate me? Oh dear, you haven't been talking to Hugh, have you?"

"No. I was speaking of your mother's engagement to the marquis. Or have you an aversion to marquises?"

Davida laughed. "Hardly, and the engagement is pleasing, to be sure."

Lady Susan had expected raptures and jubilations and eyed her subdued companion sceptically.

"You don't appear pleased."

"But I am," Davida said, pressing a pleat out of her cornflower-blue walking dress. "I am just being hen-witted, because..."

"It isn't that odious brother of mine, is it?" Susan asked.

Davida shook her head. For once Lyall was not the problem.

"If I can be of any help, my dear..." Lady Susan offered kindly.

Davida had been feeling the need to confide in someone who knew what love and marriage were all about, and did not need to be coaxed further. Moments later she was spilling out the whole tale of Hugh's offer. Lady Susan sat, her lips tilting upward in a smile that reminded Davida of her brother.

"An offer from Hugh. I am not surprised. When did it occur?"

"Last evening. I know I should have just said 'yes' or 'no' and have done with it, but I couldn't. I managed to ask him for time to reflect on the matter. Luckily, he is so understanding."

Lady Susan chewed on her lower lip and nodded encouragingly.

"You have known him so long," Davida continued. "Do you think he would make a good husband?"

"Oh, quite. Hugh is the devoted sort, no danger of straying, and one cannot forget his fortune and impeccable background. Yes, he would make a good husband for most any lady. But you—'' she directed a fond smile at Davida ''—are not just any lady, and with all your talk of Hugh and his offer, you have not mentioned love.''

Davida coloured. ''That's because I'm not sure if what I feel is love,'' she admitted. ''I know I enjoy Hugh's company, and we are quite comfortable together. At least,'' she amended, ''we never fly into disagreeable arguments.''

Lady Susan favoured her with yet another keen glance. ''Yes, diplomacy has a way of smoothing out a man's rough edges. But there can be something attractive about rough edges at times.''

Being a wise woman she said no more, and Davida was still mulling over her advice as their carriage turned in at the Baughs' residence.

Lady Baugh, a tall, thin, nervous woman, hurried out to greet her old friend, trailed by several pugs, who yapped at her heels, and four noisy children, who probably accounted in no small measure for their mother's nervousness.

The four younger children were overseen by their eldest sister, Miss Ernestine Baugh, a good-humoured nineteen-year-old who succeeded in shooing them off to an upstairs room. A short time later she, Lady Baugh, and the two visitors were sitting in the drawing room absorbed in the latest *on dits*, including the details of the wedding of Princess Charlotte to her Leopold not a month previous.

''I wonder if it will last?'' Lady Baugh said from one end of the Hepplewhite couch. ''It was not long ago that she threw over the Prince of Orange without so much as a by-your-leave, enraging poor Prinny in the process. He had selected him for her himself.''

Lady Susan nodded. ''Yes, I recall that. And there was that curious infatuation she had with Frederick. But young girls are so prone to their quirks, and fortunately, nothing came of that." She took a sip of her tea and went on. "Charlotte seems quite devoted to Leopold, and goodness knows the child deserves some happiness with two such parents as she has been forced to endure. Besides," she concluded, "it must last. Marriage is forever."

To Davida there was something telling in Lady Susan's last remark, and as the other ladies swept on to discuss in lavish detail the Oldenburg hats now sweeping the ton, she tried to envision herself tied forever to Hugh on his Kent estates. Instead of the glow of satisfaction that should be filling her heart, she felt only a mounting panic.

"Miss Cooper?" Miss Baugh's quiet words interrupted her thoughts. The younger woman was gazing at her with some concern. "Are you feeling at all the thing?"

"Oh, yes," she said quickly, realizing that the conversation had nothing more to do with Oldenburg hats but was now centring on the Prince of Orange.

"I wonder if Hugh met him, for they were both on staff to Wellington. I must remember to ask him," Lady Susan said at one point.

Miss Baugh looked surprised. "Are you referring to Mr. Hugh Sylvester?"

"Why, yes, didn't you hear he was back?"

"Does he have many thrilling tales to tell you about the Continent?" Miss Baugh demanded.

"Too many," Lady Susan said frankly. "But I'm sure he will tell you all of them if you only let him."

Davida laughed, but Miss Baugh enthusiastically reported that she for one looked forward to any tale Mr. Hugh Sylvester might deign to relate to her.

"And she might very well enjoy his tales," Lady Susan said with a shudder after she and Davida were back in the carriage. Her gloved hand hid a tiny yawn. "I must remember to speak to Hugh about Ernestine. She would be so thrilled by a visit from him. And if I don't remember *you* must mention it to him, Davida. I daresay you shall have more occasion to see and talk to him than I."

"I suppose so," Davida said, wondering why her spirits should sink at the merest mention of Mr. Hugh Sylvester coming to call.

CHAPTER THIRTEEN

BEFORE RETURNING to Upper Wimpole Street, Lady Susan took Davida on yet another call to one of the friends she had encountered at the fair earlier in the week.

"I know you will like Chloe," Susan said, giving her groom the direction to Lady Foxborough's residence.

"Is she a very good friend of yours?" Davida asked.

"Not a bosom bow exactly," Lady Susan conceded, "but really the most engaging of women. Married above herself, or so the gossip goes, but no one who knows her would care a fig about it. Her background is the theatre."

From the few details Susan supplied, Davida had conjured up an image of their hostess as a supple wraith who might have fitted the part of Mr. Shakespeare's Ophelia. Although it was true Lady Foxborough in her youth had essayed this role and found it markedly inferior to her own favourite, Juliet, declaring that it was more gratifying to die onstage of poison than offstage of drowning, her figure had grown considerably since those salad days. She was now, Davida saw as she stepped down from the carriage, almost Junoesque in stature but with a good-humoured cast to her plump face.

"You must call me Chloe," she said at once when Susan had introduced her. "We do not stand on ceremony here, although," she confided, "I must own that Chloe is a horrid name, and the reason why I adopted a *nom de théâtre*. You may have heard of it? Seraphima Du Bois?"

Davida felt certain that if she had heard this name before she would have remembered it, and replied that unfortunately she had not.

"Well, that is neither here nor there. Come this way, do," Lady Foxborough invited as they sidestepped an odd assortment of people cavorting about one drawing room.

Susan could not resist peering in the door. "What is happening?"

"I am rehearsing one of my theatricals," Lady Foxborough said. "And you must not look just yet, for it is not finished. We have much work to do. Would you like to be in it?" she asked her guests.

"Oh, heavens, no!" Davida said immediately.

"Susan?"

"Walter would not understand," Susan said with a touch of regret in her voice.

Lady Foxborough nodded. "Some husbands don't. Fortunately Foxborough lets me do what I want. He is off to Scotland himself at present. How he loves the country! I can't abide it. My complexion inevitably gets blotched or freckled. I remember an actor I worked with once who had several freckles, and a very good thing he wore rouge, for I would not have been responsible for my actions."

Davida blinked as she entered Lady Foxborough's drawing room. It appeared that their hostess shared the Regent's love of things Oriental since the room was furnished in the Eastern motif with bamboo scrolls, an ornate Chinese screen, and a red dragon on the ceiling.

Over brimming glasses of lemonade Davida learned all about the theatrical Lady Foxborough was mounting, which included the staging of *Romeo and Juliet* itself.

"Not all of it," Lady Foxborough said in answer to Susan's query. "We would need more time for that. But we will enact the important scenes. I don't think Mr. Shakespeare would mind. By all I have read about him he was a most accommodating person." She paused to sip some lemonade. "How is your brother Lyall? I think we might be able to use him in the theatrical."

Lady Susan spluttered half her lemonade into her glass. "Good heavens, Chloe. You know Jeremy would not step foot onto a stage after what happened before."

"What happened before?" Davida asked.

"He turned cat in the pan," Susan said complacently.

Davida could not believe it.

"Stage fright, they call it. He thought it a mere trifle to step out in front of people and recite his lines." She chuckled. "He found out differently. He froze."

Lady Foxborough laughed. "Poor Lyall. Do you know him?" she asked Davida.

"Too well."

"Davida and Jeremy have been at dagger points since their first meeting," Susan explained.

"Oh?" Lady Foxborough looked astonished. "I would think quite the opposite. You're just the sort of female that Lyall would take an interest in. And I should think that he would attract some measure of interest from you."

"Well, he hasn't," Davida stated emphatically. "He's high-handed and infuriating."

"Davida has another suitor more agreeable to her," Susan drawled.

Lady Foxborough looked sceptical. "Someone better than Lyall? Pray, who is it?"

"Not better, precisely, just different from him," Davida said. "Mr. Hugh Sylvester."

"Sylvester?" Lady Foxborough exclaimed. "I once knew a Sylvester. Adolphus Sylvester. Always did have the worst taste in dress. He would wear the most eye-blinding colours."

"That's Hugh's uncle," Lady Susan said. "And Hugh happily has inherited none of the tendency toward colours that his uncle loved."

"Thank God for that. And what is he like?"

"Perfectly amiable and good-natured," Davida said.

"Yes, the type of man who always does what he is told," Lady Susan added, exchanging a knowing look with her hostess.

"Sounds just like his uncle," Lady Foxborough said with a nod.

To Davida's relief the two ladies then dropped the topic of Hugh and returned to the more pleasant one of the theatre. By the end of the visit Davida had no compunction about accepting Chloe's invitation to her theatrical later in the week. If her mother fought shy of accompanying her she knew Cassie would jump at the chance.

By the time Lady Susan deposited Davida at Upper Wimpole Street it was late afternoon, and she desired nothing more than a wash and perhaps a brief nap before dinner. Unfortunately, as she entered her residence, John came forward with the look that heralded an unwelcome visitor.

"Not Cousin Henry," she protested. "I vow I haven't the time or inclination to listen to him today."

"It is not Mr. Brakeworth, Miss Davida," the servant said, "it's Mr. Sylvester. He called this morning, and again earlier this afternoon. He has been waiting for half an hour, even though I told him I had no idea when you'd return."

And she supposed it would be *de trop* to have him cool his heels much longer. She longed for the chance to tidy herself, but then decided that if Hugh was so desirous of seeing her, he must take her as she was.

She went into the sitting room where she found Hugh thumbing idly through the copies of *La Belle Assemblée* that Cassie had left strewn about.

"Hugh? John tells me you've been waiting for me. I beg your pardon, you should not have. I was out with Lady Susan."

"Yes, I know, but I didn't mind," he said, putting down the magazine. "You look wonderful."

"Only you would think so, for I vow that my throat feels full of dust. But since you have waited so long, I didn't wish to prolong your visit."

She sat down on the couch, the very same one, she realized nervously, that he had proposed on the previous day.

"Well, my dear?" he asked, when they were once again seated there. "You have had the night to contemplate your decision. What is it to be?"

His manner was so expectant that Davida felt a perfect wretch for her indecision. "Oh, Hugh, my answer is the same as it was yesterday. I don't know yet."

Hugh appeared puzzled by this unforeseen display of missishness. "But surely you must know by now, Davida. I have given you more than twenty-four hours."

"Yes," she acknowledged, unable to look him straight in the eye. "I realize that, and I am grateful. But that is really not much time, not when I must think over such an important matter."

Hugh looked more wooden than ever. "It would be quite long enough, I should think," he said stiffly, "if you were weighing the matter carefully."

"I have been weighing it carefully," she retorted. "And I should like some additional time to reflect, perhaps," she warned, "as much as a week." She shifted the brunt of her argument slightly. "I would have thought a diplomat such as yourself would know the importance of clear thinking at a time like this."

"Of course I am aware of such things," Hugh said, nettled by her words, which appeared to question his competence in the field of diplomacy.

"Good, then we are agreed I shall have more time to think on the matter." She pressed on, informing him that she had met a delightful childhood friend of his, Miss Baugh.

Hugh frowned, his look as good as implying that Davida must have invented such a person in order to put off the decision on marrying him.

"Of course, you know her," Davida answered, feeling cross. "Lady Susan said you were accustomed to playing with her when she was a child. She must be all of nineteen, blonde, blue eyed, with a rosebud mouth and a rather sweet disposition, Miss Ernestine Baugh."

"Oh, you mean Ernie," Hugh volunteered after these clues had been furnished. "Can she really be nineteen? I'm delighted you have met her, but I cannot think how she has anything to do with this conversation." Squaring his shoulders, he prepared to put his fate once more to the touch.

Davida, seeing these signs, forestalled him by moving away just as he leaned toward her to pull her to his bosom. This caused him to sprawl forward across the couch just as Lyall entered the room. The latter stood in the doorway with quizzing glass to one eye, regarding them both with marked appreciation.

"I beg your pardon, Miss Cooper, Hugh."

"And well you might," Davida snapped. "What right do you have to break in here and interrupt us?"

"It was wrong of me, I admit," Lyall said, "knowing how you treasure such private moments with Hugh."

"No!" she exclaimed as he turned his back. "I mean, well, since you've interrupted us, what do you want?"

"I came to return your Byron to you," he said promptly, holding out the book. "Cassie assured me that it would be all right to come in."

"Your sister," Hugh said, in accents of loathing.

"A bit high-spirited, young Cassie," Lyall conceded indulgently, taking a seat opposite them.

Hugh glared, but his old friend continued to speak blandly of poets, and after a few moments Hugh was forced to take his leave.

"You are without doubt the most high-handed, interfering gentleman I have ever met," Davida said heatedly, rounding on Lyall when Hugh had finally departed. "If I desire a private chat with Hugh, that is my business."

"No doubt, but any fool could see you did not desire a private chat with him! And really you should thank me. I got rid of him, didn't I?"

Reluctantly she was forced to admit to herself that Lyall had done what she had not been able to. But she would die before admitting such a fact to him.

"If you will excuse me, I have been on calls with your sister and feel in need of a rest."

"As you wish." He bowed. "I shall see you tonight."

"Tonight?"

"Lady Aldyth was kind enough to invite Lord Alwyn and me to dine this evening."

"I didn't think that you and the marquis would be boon companions, owing to the difference in age and temperament."

"You are right, but my father has asked me to keep Alwyn entertained. Papa has departed for Lord Timothy's estate to see to that precious bay of his. So in his absence I am at the marquis's disposal."

"Very obliging of you."

His eyes twinkled. "I am an obliging fellow, and you must admit that it would behoove me to keep close to Alwyn's side."

"Why? He is not decrepit, or is he?" she asked, worried.

"It is not decrepitude that I worry about as much as, let us say, an accident. He's not married to Aldyth yet, and until he is I am not safe."

"Safe from me?" she asked, nettled at his words.

"Safe from that contract," he amended. "Or have you decided to do right by Hugh and accept his offer?"

She looked up at him quickly, finding nothing in his eyes but bland interest. "How do you know he made me one?" she asked, angry at herself as much as him. "Has Cassie spoken to you?"

"Not about an offer from Hugh. But do you take me for a flat? From that tender scene I interrupted it was obvious he was making a declaration. He's not the sort to offer a lady like you carte blanche."

"Well, you are wrong," she retorted. "The offer was made yesterday."

"Really? After the fair, you mean? Well, he certainly did not let the grass grow under his feet. What does your mama say?"

"Mama doesn't know. You are not to tell her. Promise me."

"I seem to be promising you a good many things, Miss Cooper," he complained. "But don't worry, I'm true blue and shall never stain. You have always seemed to be the sort of female who had no difficulty making a decision, and yet you seem to need time to answer Hugh. Why is that, do you suppose?" he asked archly.

She glared at him, wishing she could banish that amused glint from his eyes. "Naturally one does not undertake such an important matter as marriage on a mere whim!"

"Naturally," he said, looking so smug that she exited the room before she gave in to the temptation to box his ears.

CHAPTER FOURTEEN

DAVIDA HAD NOT EXPECTED to enjoy dinner with Lyall present, but she found him on his best behaviour, offering, when asked, his opinion to the marquis and Lady Aldyth on their various plans. Indeed, Davida could not fault him at all until she overheard him urging the marquis to marry Aldyth as soon as possible. She assumed he was mindful that the sooner Aldyth was married, the sooner his tie to Davida would be dissolved.

"What do you want us to do?" Alwyn protested. "Elope?"

"That would be romantic," Cassie put in. "On the run to Gretna Green."

"I think at our age people would think we were queer in the attic if we did any such thing," Lady Aldyth said frankly. "But do have a look at this sketch of a wedding gown, Alwyn. Fanchon made it for me this morning."

She passed the drawing over to the marquis. But Lyall could not resist peeking at it, and soon they were all exchanging opinions about the fashions that ladies had adopted through the years.

"For my part I think that those patches were the worst!" Lyall declared.

"No worse than the powdered hair some gentlemen adopted," Aldyth returned.

"Are you having Weston draw something special for your wedding suit?" Lyall asked the marquis.

"Should I? What do you think, Davida, Cassie? Am I a fashionable enough swell to be allowed to marry your mother?"

"As long as you don't wear red necessaries to the wedding I shall be satisfied," Cassie said, sparking a quick outcry from her mother.

"Cassie!" she implored.

"Wherever did you hear of red necessaries?" Lyall asked, his shoulders quaking.

"It doesn't matter," Davida said. "That is more than enough about such a thing. Anyone listening would think you a veritable hoyden, Cassie."

"Sometimes I wonder what I did for amusement before I met you Coopers," Lyall said.

"I don't think you ever lacked for amusement on any horizon, my lord, particularly the female one."

"Now that is quite false," Lyall protested. "I have been obliged to pass a good many lonely hours without, as you phrase it so delicately, female companionship looming on the horizon."

"Yes," Cassie agreed. "Gentlemen get tired of their ladybirds now and then, you know!"

"Cassie!" Davida threw up her hands. "Mama," she appealed for help from Lady Aldyth.

Aldyth, chuckling herself, recovered her countenance and bade her younger daughter to act with some semblance of dignity.

"For even though Alwyn has offered for me, you know that he might think better of being attached to females such as ourselves and withdraw his offer, and then where would I be?"

"He can't do that," Cassie said. "Gentlemen are not allowed to cry off. That is the unwritten law."

But unwritten law or not, Davida thought as she went up to bed that evening, perhaps Lyall was right and the sooner Alwyn got married to her mother the better.

THE MARQUIS AND LADY ALDYTH felt under no compunction to announce their coming alliance, and derived considerable amusement from the perusal of the columns in the papers, which still linked Exley with Aldyth.

"And I hope Papa does not have an attack of the apoplexy when he returns to London and finds they are still bandying his name about," Lyall informed his sister over lunch one day at Hill Street.

Lady Susan airily waved off his concern. "Papa was only livid when there was a remote possibility that he might have to marry Aldyth. Now that the marquis has won her, he's bound to get a chuckle out of it."

"That is coming it a trifle brown," Lyall said dampeningly. "These columnists! If I ever meet up with the fellow who writes that page!"

Susan gave him a sympathetic look over the rim of her coffee cup. "Walter did say you were the target of the Bond Street beaux. Nothing too unbearable, I hope?"

He shook his head. "Just a nuisance."

"Well, perhaps they will soon quiz Hugh instead of you."

"Hugh?" he asked, his fork midway to his mouth.

"Yes, Davida received an offer from him. Surely you must have heard."

"Oh, that."

"Is that all you have to say about it? Aren't you the least bit surprised?"

"Surprised? Hardly. He's been sitting in her pocket these past few days. Danced with her three times at the Sefton ball. As for saying anything about their probable match, whenever I broach the topic of Hugh to Miss Cooper she becomes testy."

"Oh, do stop being so gudgeonish, Jer. Do I need to put the matter to you bluntly? Do you want Hugh to marry Davida?"

"I have nothing to do with it," he protested. "If she wants him let her accept his offer."

His sister put down her cup. "Lyall," she said with pointed authority. "You are a block!"

He was on the verge of uttering a withering retort when she silenced him with a hand. "Listen, do you hear that noise?"

The noise turned out to be the earl, who had returned to London with the bay and had driven over to show it off to his son. Alwyn bore him company on his own horse.

"I don't know why you want my opinion, Papa," Lady Susan protested later as she examined the horse at the earl's request. "I know nothing about horses."

"Well, I do, and this is an excellent specimen," Lyall said, putting down his glass. "I can well understand why you hounded Lord Timothy."

"I didn't hound him," the earl protested, "that was Alwyn's doing." He smiled at his friend. "By the by, Timothy says the match with Veaseley's son is settled! He sends his thanks."

"That was quick work," Lyall commented.

"Some men see what they want and go after it," Susan said in an undertone.

Lyall repressed a retort. Of late his sister had begun to grate on his nerves.

"You seem to have solved everyone's problems, sir," Lyall said to the marquis.

"Not everyone's," Alwyn demurred. "There is a little matter that perhaps you can advise me on. It concerns Miss Cooper," he said.

Intrigued, Lyall led him off to his bookroom where they remained closeted for some twenty minutes of vigorous conversation.

"DAVIDA, ARE YOU FEELING at all the thing?" Lady Aldyth's concerned voice broke into her daughter's reverie.

Davida looked up, startled. They had been sitting together discussing bridal fashions, and her mind must have drifted away.

"What did you say, Mama?" she asked apologetically.

"I asked if you were feeling ill?" Lady Aldyth said, laying one maternal hand on her daughter's brow. "You don't feel feverish."

"I'm not."

"But it's plain to see that you're out of sorts. I wonder if it is that grippe that has been spreading in town. It is supposed to make one feel weak and naggy."

"Good heavens, have I been naggy?" Davida asked contritely.

"No more than your usual," Lady Aldyth said. "But it's plain that you are a trifle out of sorts. What is the matter, my dear?"

Davida gazed into her mother's eyes, feeling guilty that Lady Aldyth should be so concerned.

"It's Hugh."

"Hugh?" Lady Aldyth sat back. "What about him?"

"He made me an offer."

"When did this take place?" her mother demanded.

"Two days ago. It wasn't at all what I'd expected."

"I suppose he didn't have the presence of mind to get to his knees," Lady Aldyth mused. "Neither did Alwyn, now that I think of it, but Hugh is much younger than the marquis and could very well get a knee down to the floor."

Davida laughed. "I don't mean that. I don't much care what position he was in when he made the offer. I'm not of as romantic a frame of mind as you and Cassie."

"Every female is a romantic, my dear," her mother chided. "But go on, what about Hugh?"

"That's it," Davida said. "He made me an offer, and Cassie broke in on us."

"If Cassie broke in on you, I can well imagine the result," Lady Aldyth said dryly. "But what did you say to Hugh?"

"I told him I needed time to think about the match," Davida replied. "And yesterday he asked for my decision."

"And you said—?" Lady Aldyth asked with feverish anticipation.

"I told him I didn't know yet."

"Ah."

"Mama, I never thought I would be such a ninnyhammer."

"Love often makes the most practical female idiotish," her mother said kindly.

"Do you think I should marry him?"

"Heavens, Davida, I have nothing to say about it. You must follow your heart. Listen to what it says."

"That sounds like good advice, Mama," Davida agreed. "But I have been trying to listen to it for the past two nights. I vow I didn't get a wink of sleep. My heart is a muddle."

"Then you must sort it out before you give Hugh an answer," Lady Aldyth said firmly. "Take all the time you must, my dear. I'm sure Hugh will understand."

To Davida's surprise, Hugh did understand, or at least he did not press her for an answer when he called that afternoon to drive her in the park. It was in the park that they encountered Miss Baugh, enjoying an outing with two of her younger sisters and brothers, and Davida suggested they join them for ices at Gunter's. As the children shouted with joy and dripped their ices on themselves, Miss Baugh quizzed Hugh on his adventures on staff with Wellington.

"Is he really as formidable as they say? Did you have any hand with the campaign at Waterloo?" she demanded.

Hugh smiled. "Formidable? I suppose so, but not once you get to know him. And as for helping him with Waterloo, I did make a few suggestions."

"I knew you would!" Miss Baugh exclaimed. "Would you tell me about it?"

"Of course," Hugh said, and began a long tale about Wellington which Davida had heard at least twice. She bent down to assist one of the Baugh children, Miss Baugh having been remiss in her duty of cleaning their now strawberry-red chins.

"Davida?"

She looked up to find the marquis standing in front of her, smiling. "Lord Alwyn." She was a bit flustered to see her future stepfather. "I didn't see you when we came in."

"Not the type of place I frequent," Alwyn agreed as he bought an ice. "But I'm like Cassie in one regard. We share a sweet tooth." He looked inquiringly at the children, and she quickly explained about Miss Baugh, who was still engaged with Hugh.

"So you are practising today."

"I beg your pardon, sir?"

He drew her aside. Hugh and Miss Baugh did not appear to notice. "I know about your plan to become a governess. You would have your hands filled with children then, you know!"

"Who told you that I planned to be a governess, sir?"

"Lyall. We had a very comfortable talk this morning, he and I."

"Oh?" she said, in a tone that boded ill for that gentleman.

"He wasn't certain that you would go through with such a plan. I told him I would do everything in my power to change your mind. You will always have a home with us, Davida," he said kindly.

"Thank you, that is very kind of you."

"You will love Ireland."

"Ireland," she repeated, made suddenly aware that her mother would be moving across the Irish Sea where Alwyn had his estates. She felt sure that Lady Aldyth would settle down comfortably enough. But could she make a similar change?

"The role of father is a new one to me," the marquis said. "I do hope I'm not poking my nose into what doesn't concern me, but I wish to help you and Cassie in any way that I can. And since in time Cassie will marry that captain of hers, when he finally does return, the bulk of my thoughts have been on you." He laughed. "I know a few Irish gentlemen who would enjoy meeting you."

She laughed, too. "I'm sure they are quite pleasant, but I do not want any of them. I am quite content with the friends I have now."

"I'm sure you are. Forgive an old man his curiosity, but which one is it to be?"

Davida looked at him in bewilderment. "I beg your pardon?"

He winked. "Is it Lyall? Or Sylvester over there? Can't say I'm surprised. As long as it's not Jeffries!"

Davida flushed crimson. "I fear you misunderstood, sir. Lyall hasn't made me an offer, and while Hugh has, I have not yet accepted. As for Sir Edwin, he has fallen for someone completely ineligible, or so his mother was saying to mine the other night."

"Ballet dancer," Alwyn confirmed.

A cry from one of the young Baughs interrupted their tête-à-tête, and Miss Baugh, recalled to her duties as elder sister, guiltily settled the squabble.

"What a remarkable woman," Davida commented to the marquis, wondering if she would be able to handle her future charges without any fuss and botheration.

But no sooner had one quarrel been settled than another reared its head.

"It's your carriage," Miss Baugh explained to Hugh after investigating the cause of the uproar. "Denis and Carlotta want to ride home in it. I told them there is no room for us."

"But of course there is," Alwyn said. "I am on my way to Upper Wimpole Street. May I escort you home, Davida?"

"There, that is the solution," Davida agreed. "The marquis will take me up. Why don't you take Carlotta and Donald into your carriage, Hugh?"

"Denis," Miss Baugh corrected with a grateful smile as she handed first one child and then the next into the hands of Hugh.

"Were you really on your way to see Mama?" Davida asked Alwyn as she settled back in his vehicle.

"Certainly. You don't think I would lie about an errand like that do you?" His eyes twinkled. "Does Aldyth know about your plans to become a governess?"

"Oh, no!" Davida said, alarmed. "And pray, don't tell her, please. She's bound to think it freakish of me, particularly since I just told her today about Hugh's offer."

The marquis's eyes twinkled again in amusement. "My lips are sealed. We can't have her thinking that it was Hugh's offer that drove you to become a governess," he said, chuckling at the idea.

Davida laughed along with him. She had always held Alwyn in the respect that his rank deserved, but now she was growing to like him very much.

In due course the carriage arrived at Upper Wimpole Street, just as Lyall's was pulling up.

"Your other suitor comes to call," Alwyn said to Davida, who coloured. If the marquis only knew how little Lyall cared for her, she thought.

Lyall, who had alighted first and was standing outside the door, held up a hand to Davida, who had no recourse but to accept his aid as she stepped down.

"Miss Cooper makes a timely return," the marquis said to Lyall. "It wouldn't do to keep you waiting."

Davida flushed but Lyall looked unperturbed.

"Quite true, sir. But in this instance it is Cassie I am calling on."

"Cassie?" Davida could not help blurting out.

"Yes, she sent the most addled message to Berkeley Square, demanding that I come here at once. I only hope her captain hasn't returned to run a sword through me. When I think of the tales she has written to him—" He stopped as the door opened and Cassie herself flew down the stairs.

"Oh, Lord Alwyn. I'm so glad you are here. And Lyall!"

"Cassie, what is going on?" Davida demanded.

Her sister's eyes widened. "Oh, Davida. It's the worst you might imagine. Cousin Henry and the Runners are here. They are going to arrest Mama!"

CHAPTER FIFTEEN

FOR A MOMENT Davida stared at her sister, wondering if Cassie had gone mad, a view evidently shared by Lyall, who gently took Cassie by the hand.

"Pray, don't excite yourself, Cassie. It is all this racketing about the city that has unhinged you."

"I am not unhinged," Cassie declared, snatching her hand away. "Mama is in the sitting room with the Runners. See for yourself!"

The three took her up immediately on this suggestion, with Davida leading the way into the sitting room. There, as Cassie had told them, they found Lady Aldyth seated on the couch, flanked by two awkward-looking men. Mr. Henry Brakeworth sat in the Trafalgar chair with a pleased smile on his lips.

"Mama, are you all right?" Davida asked, going immediately to her side. "Cassie has told us a preposterous tale of your being under arrest."

"It's no tale. It's the truth," Henry offered.

"You are a Bow Street Runner?" Alwyn asked Henry, who bristled at the mistake.

"I am not."

"Begging your lordship's pardon," the taller of the other two men said with a cough. "We're the Runners. My name is Field and this is Cummings." He pointed to his partner, who bobbed his head at the marquis.

"Then who are you?" Alwyn asked bluntly.

"My name is Henry Brakeworth. I happen to be a cousin to Lady Aldyth."

"And you are here to lend Mama your support," Davida said. She had never dreamed that she would be grateful to Henry for anything, but it just showed how much she had misjudged him. "That is good of you, cousin!"

"Davida, he is the one who is having me arrested!" Lady Aldyth exclaimed.

"What?" The marquis's eyes darkened.

"He's the one who brought the Runners here!"

"Your own cousin is sending you off to gaol?" Lyall asked incredulously.

Mr. Brakeworth flushed under the hard stares of the marquis and Lyall. But before he could say anything, Davida had linked her arm with her mother's. "If they take Mama to prison they have to take me."

"Oh, Davida, don't say that!" Lady Aldyth pleaded as Henry broke out in a bray of laughter.

"Are you Miss Davida Cooper?" Field asked, scratching his head.

"No, she is not," Lady Aldyth said at once.

"Mama, please! I certainly am Davida Cooper. Why?"

"Because, Miss, we have charges against you as an accomplice to Lady Aldyth."

"Accomplice? Accomplice to what?"

"Oh, Davida, I hoped you would be spared," her mother wailed.

"Come along," Field said, standing and taking hold of Davida's wrist. As he did so he found his own in the steely grip of Lyall.

"Release her immediately," Lyall said coldly.

Their eyes linked.

"It's official business, you mustn't interfere," Mr. Brakeworth said angrily.

"Before anyone takes Lady Aldyth anywhere someone will have to explain these charges," the marquis snapped. "And you take your hands off her daughter."

After a moment's uncertainty, Field dropped his hands.

"I didn't mean to hurt you, Miss," he said to Davida, who rubbed her wrist. The Runner, she noticed, gave his own a rub as well.

"I will explain," Henry said. "Since I am the one she hoodwinked. Last week Aldyth sold me some jewels. I paid her a thousand pounds for them. They were false. Mr. Rundell himself examined the stones." He pointed an accusing finger at his cousin. "You were out to cheat me. And it's a lucky thing I did have Rundell look the stones over, for I was set to sell the necklace myself. What a coil that would have been!"

"Aldyth, are these the stones you said you sold to pay your bill at Fanchon's?" Alwyn asked.

"Why, yes," she said. "But I didn't know they were bogus. I can't think how they could be false."

"I can," Davida said quietly. "Poor Papa must have sold the jewels and had them replaced without telling you."

"That is the likeliest solution," Lyall agreed.

"Still I find it hard to believe that Mama's own cousin would have her arrested," Davida said.

Mr. Brakeworth coloured. "I'm not acting strictly on my own behalf."

"Oh no?" Cassie hooted. "Then whose?"

"I believe I enjoy the full support of the Marquis of Alwyn on this little matter."

"What?" Lyall thundered.

"Yes, I thought that would surprise you. Aldyth is not the only one with friends in high circles. Alwyn was the one desirous of buying the gems. His man of business let fall his name. He will be quite vexed to hear that the gems are false.

I've saved him considerable time and botheration by finding out the cheat before he did."

"Then he should be grateful to you," the marquis said with a grim smile.

Mr. Brakeworth preened. "I'm sure he will, once I explain everything to him. He is said to be a man of the highest principles. He wouldn't like to be cheated and will no doubt thank me for having the presence of mind to get the jewels appraised before selling them to him."

"I think he is more inclined to throttle you," Alwyn said coldly. "For I am Alwyn."

"You're roasting me," Henry said, licking his lips.

"Hardly. Mama's going to marry him," Cassie offered.

"She's what?" The pallor on Mr. Brakeworth's face increased.

"Perhaps you don't believe me. Would you recognize my family crest?" Alwyn held out his ring to Brakeworth.

"Alwyn, do you know Henry?" Lady Aldyth asked, looking baffled.

"By Jove, no! All I did was ask my man of business to send out inquiries for those jewels you sold. I wished to restore them to you. But as for wanting you to be arrested..." The marquis shook his head, at a loss for words.

"I was just trying to do what was right," Brakeworth said hastily, "in spite of my affection for Aldyth."

"Affection!" Davida cried. "You have no affection for Mama or the rest of us. You have always been jealous of us, and I think you would have sent Mama and me to prison." She turned to Lady Aldyth. "Mama, if you don't throw Henry out, I shall!"

"Before anyone throws him out," Field said, after a nudge from his partner, "I have to remind you all that the gems were bogus and that she—" he indicated Lady Aldyth "—did take a thousand pounds for them."

"I will pay him two thousand for the necklace, bogus gems and all," Alwyn declared.

"Well, that's fair!" Henry agreed. "More than fair... I'll just drop the charges, shall I? Never let it be said that I was not of a forgiving nature," he told Aldyth, and out he skipped before anyone could make good the threat to throw him out. The Runners quickly followed.

Cassie and Davida, seeing that their mother wished to be alone with Alwyn, withdrew with Lyall to the parlour.

"Would you really have thrown him out?" Lyall asked Davida after Cassie left them to write a letter to her captain about the day's activities.

"Yes! Wouldn't you, if he were your cousin?"

"If he were my cousin, I'd be more inclined to box his ears," Lyall said dryly.

"Well, I did think of that, too," she was obliged to admit.

"This is a first for us, I believe," he said. "We have been in each other's company for at least an hour and have not come to dagger points."

"Come to think on it, there is a matter I must speak to you about," she said, her smile changing to a frown. "What did you mean by telling Alwyn I wanted to be a governess?"

"Have you changed your mind then?"

"Whether I have or have not is none of your concern. You had no right to tell Alwyn my plans for the future. You promised me that you would not."

"I promised you that I would not tell your mother," Lyall said, stung by her words. "And I didn't mean to let fall the information, but he was very concerned about you and your future plans and whether you would take to Ireland. To ease his mind I mentioned that I could vouch for your future plans." He grimaced. "For a few moments he thought that meant that you and I—"

"Naturally you set him to rights on that point," she said coldly.

"Of course. And that meant explaining your future plans as a governess. Not that I think you will make a good governess."

"And why not?" she demanded tartly. "I have the education, I assure you."

"I know. You are also full of that precious commodity of pride, with your nose, pretty as it is, so high in the air when you take umbrage at me. It's rather amusing in a lady of quality but hardly what one wants in a governess."

"And what do you know about governesses?"

"Very little," he conceded. "But I have a few acquaintances who are married and blessed with offspring. I can put in a word for you."

"You are very obliging."

"Yes, I know. Although in strict conscience I ought to point out that you have an alternative to a life as a drudge in someone's household, by accepting friend Hugh's offer. Or has he fallen short of the mark of what you desire in a husband?"

Davida's eyes flashed in anger. "I happen to think Hugh is an exceedingly kind, amiable gentleman who would make any lady a splendid husband."

Lyall yawned delicately. "I was up rather late last evening," he explained. "And you should by rights be saying this to Hugh. I am doubly certain that he is yearning to hear all this and more from your lips. I find it amazing how his eyes mirror his yearning, don't you think?"

"I had not noticed, my lord," Davida said frostily.

"Then you have been remiss," Lyall scolded. "I thought you the type of lady who would notice the eyes of her beloved. Hugh has certainly been noticing you. When he does so, his eyes put me greatly in mind of those of a hound gazing at a bone."

With some difficulty Davida swallowed her laugh. "You are preposterous. I have no intention of hearing you slight Hugh any further."

"You are quite right," Lyall said equably. "Not a hound at all, more like a spaniel."

"If you say another word about dogs, Lyall..." Davida threatened.

He laughed and took his leave, waving her adieu after he climbed into his carriage. Against her will she waved back.

Upstairs she found Cassie still writing to Bruce. Cassie was certainly devoted to her captain, Davida thought as she sat down. Just as their mother was growing devoted to Alwyn. Would it ever be possible for her to become similarly entranced with Hugh? Davida wondered. Or was that nothing but an air dream?

"Has Lyall gone, then?" Cassie asked, looking up at last to see her sister with a faraway look in her eyes.

"Yes," Davida said quietly. "Lyall has gone."

CHAPTER SIXTEEN

THE QUESTION OF HUGH'S OFFER began to feel to Davida much like an aching tooth. Someday she would have to tend to it, but for the moment she was too occupied in enjoying the simple pleasures of London. She was grateful that Hugh did not press her during his daily calls at Upper Wimpole Street, having apparently accepted her request for more time to think.

Had he been any other man—Lyall for some reason came to mind—he would have badgered her out of patience within the hour. But Hugh was not Lyall. And yet, even his powers of patience, honed in the fires of diplomacy, might dissipate entirely if she continued to behave so missishly.

On Wednesday morning, however, Hugh betrayed no signs of impatience as he helped Davida into his barouche for the trip to Lady Foxborough's theatrical. Davida, wearing a honey-coloured frock and matching chip hat, was prepared to enjoy herself, but as she had no wish to engage in a prolonged tête-à-tête with Hugh she had coaxed Cassie into coming with them to the theatrical. Lady Aldyth had previously accepted Susan's offer of transport.

Cassie was only too happy to fall in with Davida's scheme, for she had been growing more and more alarmed by Hugh's continued courtship of Davida. At first she was certain that Davida would refuse him out of hand, but as the days went by and no decision was rendered—a fact that teased her nearly as much as it must have Hugh—she wondered if Davida was in fact seriously considering accepting his proposal.

That would never do. Not that Hugh was not unfailingly civil and amiable to her, but she much preferred Lyall, and she half suspected that Davida did too, and was just too proud to admit it.

Perhaps, Cassie thought, as Hugh drove along the North Road from London, she would do better to scotch the match by appealing to Lyall. But there, too, she admitted, there were obstacles to success. Lyall was nearly as stubborn as Davida!

She pondered the matter as Hugh chatted across to Davida, inquiring whether Exley would be in attendance at the theatrical.

"No. Lyall said that he is planning to enter one of his Arabians in a race. So he is making certain that all is well on that score."

"I should like to go to the race," Cassie said.

"You?" Hugh laughed.

"What is wrong with attending a horse race?" she demanded.

"I don't know. It's just rather odd for a female, don't you think?"

"I was used to attending much odder places," Cassie said. "Once Papa took me to a boxing mill!"

"Cassie!" Davida cautioned, certain that Hugh would think them sunk beneath reproach. His amiable expression did not fully mask the surprise reflected in his eyes. "That is more than enough about odious boxing mills!"

"I wasn't going to talk about boxing mills," Cassie said. "I was talking about horse races. Don't you remember you went to one once and said it was the best time you ever had?"

"Yes, and I also am trying to remember just how we must find Bright Wood," she said, changing the subject.

"Oh, you needn't worry there," Hugh said quickly. "Lady Foxborough gave me the directions."

Unfortunately, the directions Lady Foxborough had provided Hugh were in no way adequate, for after an hour in strange terrain he was obliged to admit he was lost.

"Lost!" Cassie expostulated. "How could you be lost!" Lyall, she was sure, would never be lost in his life.

"These directions are not in order," Hugh explained, his patience sorely tried by having Cassie in his vehicle.

"We shall probably miss the performance of *Romeo and Juliet*," Cassie said mournfully. "Lady Foxborough told me that it was bound to be a spectacular."

"We shall certainly see something at the theatrical," Davida soothed, "for it will run all day, and I'm sure that no performance ever started on time. Hugh, do you think if we went back along this road toward the fork and took the branch to the left, it might lead us to Bright Wood?"

"We could try that," he said grudgingly, looking for a place to turn his team around. A half hour later they were at the fork, but after another half hour they were forced to admit that they were just as lost as before.

Ordinarily, being lost would have been an adventure to Cassie, but today with the theatrical going on, her mood turned peevish.

"This would never have happened if Lyall were driving," she said, crossing her arms on her chest as Hugh continued to search for a familiar landmark.

"Lyall!" Davida exclaimed. "What has Lyall to do with this!"

"Nothing!" Cassie replied. "He is a top sawyer, everyone knows. A member of the Four Horse Club. I don't suppose you are a member, Hugh?"

This privilege had been denied Mr. Sylvester by reason of the fact that he had spent the past four years on the Continent, but the reminder did nothing to improve his temper.

"Unfortunately, Lyall did not offer to drive you and your sister," he pointed out crushingly. "I did. Or rather, I offered to drive your sister."

"And I am grateful to you, Hugh," Davida said. "Look, there is someone coming down the road. Do you think he might be able to direct us to Bright Wood?"

The person in question was a vicar, who seemed amused at their being lost.

"If you would just give us direction, Reverend," Hugh said testily, after explaining their predicament.

"If it's Bright Wood you want, you must go back along the road east." The vicar pointed the way. "It's about five miles, then take the south fork. You'll find the estate ten minutes after the fork."

"Thank you," Davida said.

"Not at all," the vicar said, chuckling. "Lost!"

Hugh, in no way pleased at being made an object of fun by a vicar, lost no time in following his directions.

"There's the fork!" Cassie pointed out. "Take the south one."

"I know. I heard the vicar," Hugh replied, even as he made the turn.

"You also heard Lady Foxborough," Cassie said. "And see what happened."

"Nothing has happened," Davida said, regretting that she had ever asked Cassie along. She must have had windmills in her head! "We are just a trifle late."

Finally, to everyone's relief, they came to the pines that gave Bright Wood part of its name, and then after five more minutes spent tooling up the driveway, they had arrived.

Lady Foxborough, dressed in a Chinese-red day dress and turban, bustled over to them, followed by a young lady in French muslin.

"My dears, where have you been? We were getting quite worried!" Lady Foxborough exclaimed.

"We were just delayed," Davida said, recognizing the young lady as Miss Baugh.

"Because Hugh got lost!" Cassie murmured.

Hugh reddened.

"These country roads are so badly marked I'm not surprised you got lost," Miss Baugh said. "That has happened to my father any number of times."

"Is he a member of the Four Horse Club?" Cassie asked.

"Well, no," Miss Baugh conceded.

"It doesn't matter, we are here now," Davida pointed out.

"Yes," Lady Foxborough declared. "And just in time. The performance will take place in ten minutes at the Pavilion." She pointed them toward the building. "I bade Lyall save you seats!"

Cassie needed no further urging to get to the Pavilion, and she skipped on ahead, trailed by Davida, Miss Baugh, and Hugh, who would much rather have had a cool drink than be obliged to listen to any group of actors. Fortunately Miss Baugh managed to coax him out of his dismals by asking about the roads in Europe during the war, which had the desired effect of sparking a reminiscence of the Iron Duke.

Cassie led the way to the seats Lyall had reserved, and in no time Davida found herself seated between Lyall and Hugh, with Miss Baugh on Hugh's other side. Lady Susan was also in the party.

"Have we missed anything?" Cassie demanded.

"Just a few scenes of *Hamlet* and *A Midsummer Night's Dream*," Lady Susan said. "*Romeo and Juliet* is next."

"Good." Cassie heaved a sigh of relief. "We'd have been here from the start were it not for Hugh's—"

"Encountering so much traffic on the road," Davida said, directing a quelling look at Cassie. She had said enough about Hugh's getting lost.

"Lady Foxborough did invite a good many guests," Susan agreed, while Lyall's mocking eyes flitted across Hugh's reddened face. "I thought I saw Lady Jersey here this morning."

"Really?" Davida asked.

"In the front." Lyall nodded toward the first row of chairs. "She's wearing that hat with the ostrich plume! And no one has the courage to tell her to remove it."

Davida laughed. "Perhaps I should remove my hat," she said, taking it off. Her hair spilled free onto her shoulders. "Is that better?" she asked him.

"Much better," he said simply.

The curtain rose just then on Mr. Shakespeare's young lovers, and for the next hour the audience was transported to Verona. The presentation was superb, with the two star-crossed lovers wringing many tears from the audience. Lyall was obliged to lend the tearful Cassie his handkerchief, but he himself seemed unaffected by the play and was the first to his feet when the scene ended.

"Now to the refreshments," he said, rubbing his hands with anticipation.

"Is that what brought you here today, sir?" Davida asked, applauding the actors vigorously. "The refreshments?"

"You didn't sit through three scenes of *Hamlet* and most of *A Midsummer Night's Dream*," he retorted. "Oh, no! They are going to do an encore!"

He slumped back in his chair, looking so dismayed that Davida bit back a laugh. Fortunately, the encore was merely a recitation of one of Mr. Shakespeare's sonnets, and before too long Lyall was able to lead the exodus across the lawn toward the table that Lady Foxborough had had set up.

"As though you were starving," Davida chided.

"I nearly am," he said, offering her a chicken leg, which she accepted and found so good that she took a second.

"Now who is starving?" he asked, alarmed by such traces of appetite, which promised to deplete his plate in no time.

"Well, I must own I did work up considerable appetite on the road," she conceded.

"Helped in no little case by friend Hugh getting lost?" he hazarded a guess.

"Yes, but don't tease him about that, pray."

"Of course not. I myself on my first trip to Bright Wood found the roads a veritable maze." He led her toward the glasses of lemonade. "Or would you liefer champagne?"

"Lemonade will do nicely," she said. She took a sip and the tart liquid slid down her parched throat.

"I shall take a glass of champagne," Cassie declared.

"No, you will not," Lyall said cordially but firmly, handing her a lemonade. "I shouldn't wish your captain to return from the peninsula and find you foxed!"

Cassie burst out laughing and took the lemonade. Lady Foxborough, mingling with her guests, came forward to ask if anyone would like to meet the actors. Susan and Cassie took her up on her offer.

"You do not wish to meet the illustrious actors?" Lyall asked Davida.

"No, I'd liefer another chicken leg," she divulged.

"Alas, I have only lobster patties left," he said, proffering the plate.

She took it anyway, saying that the only actor she might wish to meet was Mr. Edmund Kean.

"I met him once at a performance of *Hamlet*," Lyall divulged. "Sherry, that is Richard Sheridan, introduced us."

"What was he like?"

"Rather ordinary fellow. Very dark. Not a gentleman."

"Of whom are you talking, Lyall?" Hugh demanded, having strolled up to find Davida.

"Someone whom Davida is enamoured with," Lyall replied, the twinkle very obvious in his eyes.

"Oh?" Hugh asked.

"Mr. Edmund Kean," Davida explained quickly. "And I am not enamoured of him. Lyall is just roasting me."

"Lobster patty, Hugh?" Lyall offered.

"No. I shall get my own for Ernie—Miss Baugh, I mean," he said, heading back toward the refreshment table.

"I was wrong," Lyall said, an enigmatic expression on his dark face.

"Wrong about what, pray?" Davida asked.

"About Hugh. Not a hound or a spaniel, more of a bull-dog."

Davida choked. "If he is intransigent today it is with good reason. I had asked Cassie to accompany us, and she vexed him beyond belief in the carriage. And what is so funny?" she demanded, as he too laughed.

"I have heard of gentlemen getting lost when they wished to be alone with the woman riding with them," he said, making a recovery, "but never when the woman's sister was also with him!"

She smiled reluctantly.

"Is Hugh driving the two of you back to London?" he asked.

"Why, yes," she said, then stopped, not too pleased at the thought of the battle that would probably take place in their vehicle. "I don't relish it."

"Then let me drive Cassie back," he said.

"Would you?"

"If it will help."

"You are being very helpful to me, Lyall," she said.

"Yes, I know." He grinned. "Don't let it tease you. It is undoubtedly a freakish whim and within another day we will be back to dagger drawing. Let me just go and see if I can find Cassie and find out if she would like to drive back to London with me!"

Cassie fully approved of the plan to ride with Lyall instead of Hugh, especially since this gave her an opportunity to further Davida's cause with Lyall. But no matter how much she praised her sister through the course of the drive, Lyall did not appear to take heed.

"Don't you think I'm right, Lyall? About Davida and Hugh, I mean?"

"What about Davida and Hugh?" he asked indulgently.

"That she shouldn't marry him!"

"My dear Cassie, just because a fellow loses his way on the road, he is not disqualified from being an excellent husband."

"It's not just that," Cassie said. "Davida deserves the best."

To which Lyall, yawning, excused himself, and said that the topic had begun to bore him a trifle and might they talk instead of other matters. That put Cassie in mind of the race that Exley's horses were going to run next week, and she spent the rest of the trip back to London trying to persuade Lyall to take her to the races.

"Ask your mother," Lyall said with a laugh as he handed her down at Upper Wimpole Street.

"Mama will say no!"

"She may not," he said gently. "Remember that Alwyn's horses are running, too."

"That's right!" Cassie brightened. She hastened into the house, where Davida and Lady Aldyth stood in the hallway in animated conversation with a sandy-haired gentleman. Lyall, who was at Cassie's side, felt her stiffen and then was nearly trampled as she sprang at the visitor, shrieking: "Bruce! Bruce!"

CHAPTER SEVENTEEN

SEVERAL MOMENTS PASSED before Captain Fitzwilliam could detach Cassie's arms from what felt like a stranglehold about his neck.

"And here is Lord Lyall, Bruce," Cassie said, tugging impatiently at his sleeve and beaming at the two men.

At the mention of Lyall, the captain's grin disappeared. "I remember your mentioning his lordship in that letter you left for me in London," he said stiffly. "And perhaps you might wish to explain what you meant when you wrote that you were engaged—"

"Of course she is engaged." Lyall spoke in the polite but utterly uninterested manner of a man quite accustomed to breaking willy-nilly into any conversation he wished. "Engaged to you, that is, Fitzwilliam. She has been boring us all to tears on the subject of your return and eventual marriage. Cassie," he directed, "I believe you had better make your captain known to Susan before she expires of curiosity."

The captain, confused by Lyall's words, could not think of an adequate response, for he was being bustled over to shake hands with Lady Susan. While the others lingered in the foyer Davida went into the sitting room. Lyall followed.

"What was that all about?" she asked.

"Nothing that signifies, Miss Cooper," he assured her airily.

"With you, my lord, I find that everything signifies."

"Do you indeed?" he asked, shaking an admonishing finger at her. "If I did not know you any better, Miss Cooper, I'd call you a bluestocking. And I do hope you are not about to turn into one of their league, possessed of little but their intelligence, examining in the most scrupulous way possible the simple matters of life such as trees, stars, or love."

"I should hope not myself," Davida answered. "And to prevent such a fate from overtaking me I shall contrive to keep silent in the future on those three subjects."

"Ah, but you must speak of love when you marry Hugh," Lyall pointed out.

"I wish you would stop speaking of Hugh to me," she retorted.

Lyall dipped two fingers into his snuffbox. "I merely wished to point out to you the advantages of such a match. Hugh is a notoriously humble chap, perhaps he didn't tell you about his large income from his uncle or the very tidy competence his father left him."

"I know all about that, and his precious estates in Kent," Davida replied.

"And about Wellington, too, I daresay?" he quizzed.

She smiled. "Rather too much about him."

"I suppose Cassie's captain will have similar tales of adventure. I, for one, am glad finally to meet him. I had begun to think him a figment of her imagination. And perhaps it would have been better if he had remained so."

Alarmed, Davida glanced up. "Why on earth?"

"I had him pictured a shade more dashing," Lyall explained. "All in all he seems rather unheroic."

In justice no one could have quarrelled with Lyall's assessment, for Captain Fitzwilliam did have a deplorable lack of height. Davida, however, glad to have some safer topic to indulge in than her possible marriage to Hugh, defended the captain so spiritedly that anyone overhearing could have been forgiven for presuming it was she and not her sister who was shortly to marry him.

"The captain may lack your height, but he is quite an honourable sort," she concluded grandly to Lyall. "And I do hope you don't mean to thrust a spoke into that wheel."

"What an odd fellow you must think me," Lyall complained, enjoying the flash that anger always imparted to her eyes. "As though I enjoyed thrusting spokes into wheels. And it would have been a sheer waste of time for me to tell Cassie whom to marry. She'd turn me a deaf ear, I have no doubt."

Davida was forced to admit that this was probably so, for Cassie rarely listened to anyone, including her mother and sister.

Lyall had by this time exhausted his tepid interest in the affairs of Cassie and her captain and began to speak of Miss Baugh. So marked were his questions that Davida's curiosity was piqued. "Miss Baugh is an exceedingly lovely young lady," she said, "and very much the innocent."

Lyall, despite his sister's aspersions to the contrary, was no slow top. He glanced at Davida in perfect understanding. "You may take off that dragon face. It is not my ignoble intention to seduce young Miss Baugh, if that's what you fear. Nor," he went on, "have I the least intention of making her the object of my gallantry. My preference in that area runs quite different from naïve girls, as you should know."

Two spots of colour burned brightly in Davida's cheeks. "I do not make it a habit to acquaint myself with those females enjoying your patronage, my lord," she said freezingly.

"So you don't," he agreed. "And that does relieve me. As for Miss Baugh, I assure you I make it a habit never to seduce old friends."

Davida could not help pointing out that Miss Baugh had not seen him in years. "So she might not consider you an old friend. And your town bronze might scare her."

Lyall blinked. He had been accused of *faux pas* in the past but never of putting any young female into fright. "The last souls I endeavoured to dazzle with my town bronze," he said with a shake of his head, "were you and your charming family. And far from your being afraid of me or put into a quake by my top-lofty ways, quite the reverse took place."

Davida, remembering vividly their first meeting, chuckled. "It would have been stupid to be in a quake when one could choose to be civil instead. And did you really try and dazzle us, my lord?"

"Just once," he returned unflappably. "And since it didn't take, I did not subject myself to any further tests."

"But you did look magnificent," Davida said. "Quite the top of the trees, and I distinctly recall admiring your coat and the gloss on your Hessians." She bent now to admire them again. "Champagne, I daresay, gives them that sheen."

"Yes, according to Wilkes, who is notoriously close-mouthed on the details of my wardrobe."

"Perhaps it's just as well you didn't dazzle Miss Baugh," Davida said kindly. "I believe she has a growing *tendre* for Hugh."

Interest kindled on Lyall's face. "Is one allowed to ask how you came by this information? I know your great dislike of eavesdropping. Or can it be just one of those feelings an engaged lady gets from those also in love with her beloved?"

"What fustian!" Davida said sharply. "Hugh is not my beloved, and," she could not resist adding, "we are not engaged as yet. As for Miss Baugh, although she did not say anything specific, she did press us for all manner of details about Hugh, his time on the Continent, and his various diplomatic exploits.''

''No doubt your sex is better equipped at deducing *tendres* from such meagre evidence as that,'' Lyall murmured doubtfully, ''but it strikes me that Miss Baugh had declared nothing more than a fatal fascination for the workings of espionage, which if the war were still on would have branded her a possible Bonapartist agent, but since the hostilities are ended, we must acquit her on that account. It would have served your purpose better,'' he continued, ''to have paid attention to her eyes.''

''Her eyes?'' Davida exclaimed, her own widening at his words.

''Yes,'' he said. ''Yearning, you must know.''

''Well, I don't know if they yearned,'' Davida said, considering the matter carefully. ''But they did seem to gleam whenever she looked Hugh's way.''

To which Lyall remarked that while gleaming was passable, it could not stand ground next to yearning, but perhaps Miss Cooper did not know how to judge such things, and when he next encountered Miss Baugh he would determine this for himself. That led Davida to answer, as she left him to his billiards, that were he to do that, Miss Baugh would undoubtedly think him foxed.

THE AFTERNOON DRIFTED BY. Davida turned her attention to refurbishing a riding hat, and was trying to decide whether the new ribbon she had put on it was a complete success when Cassie waltzed into her bedchamber. Cassie had been obliged to part temporarily from her captain, to allow him to visit his own rooms for a needed wash and change of clothes.

''Mama invited him to stay with us, since it would be stupid for him to put up at a hotel. And the ride to London was so dusty,'' Cassie explained. ''He was obliged to come on horseback, which I consider excessively romantic, don't you? And he has only one satchel, which I think must have gone through every battle with him. Isn't it famous?''

Davida, still thinking of the ribbon, which did not quite match the colour of the frock she had intended it to, asked what could possibly make a satchel famous.

Cassie burst out laughing. ''Not the satchel, silly. Bruce's return. Isn't it wonderful? Haven't you been attending to a word I've said?''

''I'm sorry, Cassie,'' Davida apologized as she reached for her scissors. The ribbon would have to go. ''My mind was on other things.''

''On Hugh, I daresay?'' Cassie asked with a rather grown-up air.

Since Hugh was the last person Davida had been thinking of, she gave a guilty start, almost jabbing the scissors point into her thumb. Quickly she put them aside.

''Davida,'' Cassie asked as she watched her sister, ''have you made up your mind yet about Hugh?''

''No,'' Davida said. ''And don't you start hounding me, either. You're quite as bad as Lyall.''

''As Lyall?'' Cassie repeated, diverted by the intrusion of this name into the conversation. ''Do you mean he's been hounding you to marry him?''

''Of course not!'' Davida snapped, aghast. ''The ideas you do come up with, Cassie. I assure you that that is the furthest thing from my mind or Lyall's. He has been urging me to marry Hugh,'' she said, winding a ribbon about her finger. ''Holding forth in the most odious way possible all the advantages of such a match. Come to think on it, he is probably relieved Hugh offered for me. For if I do marry, there is not a chance that I shall enforce that stupid contract Papa left behind. He would be safe.''

''Did you intend to enforce the contract?'' Cassie asked, astonished.

"No, that was just to force him into helping us with Mama. And now, that is more than enough about Lyall. Tell me, how is your captain?"

This question diverted Cassie so successfully that for the next half hour Davida was obliged to sit through a shower of praise for Captain Bruce Fitzwilliam, which included Cassie's assurance that aside from a minor shoulder wound sustained in battle, he had come through the war in excellent fashion.

"And he's grown a moustache," she said. "He says it's the latest rage."

"It's one rage I hope does not last long," Davida replied, having her own preference for clean-shaven men. She smiled over at her sister, who was lying on her bed. "Now that Bruce is back you'll be getting married. Have you thought when that will be?"

Cassie had spent the better part of the afternoon exploring that issue with her captain. Now she shrugged. "I shall leave that to Mama."

"Then, perhaps, we ought to ask Mama," Davida said.

BUT WHEN THE MATTER was broached to Lady Aldyth later, she was even more vague than Cassie.

"I have left all my wedding plans up to Giles. The very idea of a large wedding is so fatiguing. And there is never any sense in inviting all of one's friends. And to think of you, Cassie, getting married too!" She hugged her younger daughter. "I do suppose we have to invite family." She bit her lip. "Do you think we should ask Henry?"

Davida was quite willing to face a civil war on this issue. "He brought the Runners here to arrest you," she reminded her mother.

"The only way he will attend my wedding is over my dead body," Cassie declared.

"Yes, dear, I know you dislike him so, but if you were dead we wouldn't be holding a wedding and inviting Henry," Lady Aldyth pointed out. But she gave in to her daughters' arguments and agreed that they would strike Mr. Brakeworth from their wedding list.

"A wedding should be a happy occasion," she said firmly.

"Yes, and hopefully we shall have three such happy occasions to celebrate!" Cassie added coyly.

Lady Aldyth's gaze shifted from daughter to daughter. "What? Do you mean Davida has accepted Hugh? Oh, my dear, why didn't you tell me?" she asked, embracing Davida. "I assure you I quite like Hugh, even though I had entertained hopes that you and Lyall might make a match of it."

"I haven't accepted Hugh yet," Davida said, cutting short these felicitations. "I haven't made up my mind."

"And I wasn't talking about Hugh but of Lyall," Cassie explained. "Mama, you must talk sense into Davida. Anyone can plainly see that Lyall is the better man than Hugh."

Lady Aldyth, of the opinion that the quickest way to get a lady to accept an offer was to raise all manner of objection to a suitor, bestowed a look of disapproval on her younger daughter, adjuring her not to be a flibbertigibbet.

"Davida has too much sense to accept Hugh merely because someone else tells her not to. The decision is hers." She darted a quick sympathetic look at her elder daughter. "But I daresay that Hugh will be expecting a decision soon."

To which Davida replied that she rather thought he would, and she excused herself to return to her own chamber to ponder her fate as a possible Mrs. Hugh Sylvester.

CHAPTER EIGHTEEN

WITH BRUCE'S RETURN to London, the future of at least two Cooper females seemed settled. The future of the third, however, continued to remain a vexatious muddle, as Davida herself realized. Always a practical young woman, she felt completely befuddled. Not that the question was so complex. She could accept Hugh's offer and enjoy a life as his wife on his estates in Kent, or reject him and make her own way as a governess. Pray, what else was she waiting for?

Davida's situation had not escaped Cassie's attention even though she was kept busy during the week of Bruce's return. Indeed, at times, enjoying the attention of her long-absent captain, Cassie felt a pang of guilt that she should be so happy with Bruce when all Davida had to look forward to was a life with Hugh.

She had given up all hope of talking sense into her sister. And as for Lyall, he listened to what she said with an indulgent air but said nothing in return. Clearly her past strategy had been wrong.

Instead of trying to drive Davida and Lyall together, she would work on driving Davida away from Hugh. That would be much easier to accomplish. She felt pleased with this strategy, which had come upon her as she was reading a lending-library romance. She would have liked to take Bruce into her confidence but for some reason did not think he would fully approve of her manoeuvrings. Even though Bruce had spoken to Lyall and had accepted her explanation that she had never been engaged to him, the captain did not seem to appreciate Lyall the way Cassie had hoped he would.

The first opportunity for Cassie to put her new strategy into practice occurred at the races, where Exley's and Alwyn's horses were scheduled to race. All of the Coopers were in attendance that afternoon, with Davida sporting the riding hat she had at last successfully refurbished. The day was warm with just a hint of breeze which promised it would not become insufferably hot.

She sat back in Hugh's carriage, enjoying the warmth of the sun and hoping Hugh would not get lost on the way to the Downs. Mr. Sylvester's sense of direction, however, in this case did not fail them, and his carriage reached the racing field, which was already crowded with vehicles and passengers.

Davida had packed a picnic hamper, for the events were not due to start until one. Over an assortment of cold chicken, ham, strawberries and champagne, Hugh expounded on the races ahead. She was listening to his opinions with polite interest when another voice, oddly familiar, intruded.

Glancing down from the carriage, Davida and Hugh noticed Cassie standing next to a somewhat beleaguered-looking Captain Fitzwilliam.

"Here you are, Davida," Cassie called gaily. "I have been searching the Downs for you."

"Why on earth would you do that?" Davida asked, noticing that the captain looked rather surprised at Cassie's words. "Where are Mama and the others?"

Cassie waved in the direction of a small canopy in the distance, which had been set up with chairs. "We have a much better view from there," she said. "Wouldn't you and Hugh like to join us?"

"Later, when we are finished eating," answered Davida.

"Yes, Cassie," Bruce broke in, exasperated. "Do let them eat in peace."

"But I am quite ravenous myself," Cassie said in a plaintive voice, unwilling to be so easily fobbed off and quite determined today to take a hand in Davida's affairs.

The captain, not being privy to these feelings, was utterly bewildered. "How can you possibly be hungry?" he demanded. "You just finished eating."

Cassie paid him no heed, and instead inquired of Hugh if that was a chicken leg she noticed in front of him. Hugh stared down at the drumstick in his fingers and announced that it was, indeed, and with a look of regret passed it down to her.

"Or perhaps you would like to eat it up here with us," he asked in some confusion.

Favouring Hugh with a radiant smile, Cassie accepted his halfhearted invitation and took her place on the seat opposite her sister, not appearing too alarmed at the captain, whom she left scowling down below.

"Would you like to come up, too, Bruce?" Davida asked. "Oh, you have not yet met Hugh, have you?" She hastily performed the introductions.

The captain acknowledged Hugh with a curt nod, continuing to glare at Cassie. "I'm returning to the others," he announced. "Are you coming?"

"How can I?" Cassie answered. "Don't you see I am still eating?" And she waved the drumstick in her fingers. "But you go on ahead. I shall come along later with Hugh and Davida."

The captain turned on his heel and stalked off.

Davida felt a twinge of alarm. "I don't think you should have done that, Cassie," she chided. "Bruce looked most displeased."

But Cassie, gnawing confidently on the chicken leg and accepting a sip of champagne from a glass, adjured her sis-

ter not to be a ninnyhammer and to leave the handling of
Captain Bruce Fitzwilliam to her.

SOME TWENTY MINUTES LATER they left the barouche to join
Lady Aldyth and the marquis, the Earl of Exley and his son
and daughter, and the scowling Captain Bruce Fitzwilliam.

While the earl and the marquis were absorbed in the
competition their horses would be facing, the two younger
gentlemen had been conversing politely with the ladies. But
as Cassie cheerily came up to them, Bruce fell abruptly silent, a situation that caused Davida's brow to knit.

"Oh, he always gets on his high ropes," Cassie said dismissively when Davida pointed out the captain's obvious
displeasure. "It doesn't mean a thing. And I shall certainly
cure him of that when we marry." She raised her voice now
as she asked Hugh which horse he preferred in the coming
race.

Hugh was a trifle surprised at finding himself the target
of Cassie's interest that afternoon. He replied that he would
hope she would root home Alwyn's or Exley's steeds.

Davida gave her sister a nudge toward the captain, but
Cassie ignored the vacant seat next to Bruce and flounced
over to sit by her mother. Attempting to cover up for her
sister's slight to Bruce, Davida asked, "Captain Fitzwilliam, I wonder if you would be kind enough to sit by Cassie. Spectacles of this nature always make her nervous."

The captain had never known Cassie to be nervous about
anything, but he moved obediently to the chair next to her.
She chose to ignore him still.

"Is it my imagination," Lyall drawled as Davida sat down
next to him, "or has the air hereabouts turned a trifle
chilly?"

"Arctic, I should have said," Davida murmured in turn.

Hugh, who was sweating profusely, gave them both an
odd look, then demanded of Lyall if he had enough time

before the race to pay a visit to the Baughs, whom he had noticed while escorting Cassie and Davida to their chairs.

"But of course, Hugh," Lyall answered. "You have at least ten minutes before the start of the first race," and he added unnecessarily, "I shall take good care of Miss Cooper in your absence."

"Do you mind, Davida?" Hugh asked, glancing at her.

"Oh, not at all," she answered, thinking that perhaps with Hugh out of the way, Cassie and Bruce could make up their quarrel.

Unfortunately, neither Cassie nor her captain showed the slightest inclination to communicate with each other, and by the time the first race commenced Hugh was still engaged with the Baughs. During the ensuing race Davida lost all track of Hugh, concentrating instead on cheering home the favourites. Lyall, who stood by her elbow, showed himself to be an expert judge of horseflesh.

Exley and Alwyn were flushed and jubilant with their victories.

"I'll have to find that fellow Jarvis," Exley crowed. "He owes me a hundred pounds."

"It's the Arabian strain," Alwyn declared, looking satisfied with the day's showing.

Lady Aldyth noticed Bruce was still sitting in stony silence next to Cassie. "Would you agree with that opinion, Captain Fitzwilliam?"

The captain jerked his head up and stated that he would take Arabian stock over English at any time.

"But that strikes me as unpatriotic," Cassie complained.

The captain snorted. "We're talking horses, not politics. Besides, what does a schoolroom miss like you know about horses?"

A black frown descended on Cassie's face, alarming both Davida and her mother. But Cassie merely tossed her head and turned a cold shoulder to the captain, who did not notice, for he was too occupied in turning her a cold shoulder of his own.

As the races came to a finish Davida looked about for Hugh, but the crush of people exiting the Downs made finding him a virtually impossible task. She discovered Lyall at her side, bearing her company on her search lest she be crushed to death.

"I just wonder where Hugh has gone to," she said as they dodged a running child.

Lyall shrugged. "He may have gotten lost. I can always take you home, but I daresay he might take offence at that. Ah, there he is, and still with the Baughs."

Davida was startled to find Hugh escorting Miss Baugh to the Baughs' carriage. Miss Baugh's animated expression disappeared when she saw Davida, as did Hugh's.

"Miss Cooper?" he stammered.

"Pray, don't be concerned," Davida said. "How do you do, Miss Baugh, Lady Baugh. Hugh, Lyall tells me he can see me home if you are too occupied here."

"Too occupied?" Hugh looked more strangled than ever. "Really, Miss Cooper, I don't know what you must think of me."

"Miss Cooper thinks you a splendid chap," Lyall asserted, covering the breach nicely. "But I do believe you should take her home, and I shall just have a word with the Baughs myself."

Taking this as his cue to leave Miss Baugh gracefully, Hugh offered his arm to Davida. "I do apologize, Miss Cooper. I can't imagine where the time went, and I hope I haven't given offence."

"Not at all. Why should I be offended just because you chose to speak with Miss Baugh, who I know was a particular friend of yours from childhood."

"Well, not that particular," Hugh said as they came to his barouche. He helped her in. "And we really weren't great friends as children. Ernie seemed so much younger then."

"I daresay she no longer seems so young to you?" Davida said, watching him closely.

"No, 'pon rep, she doesn't," Hugh agreed, with such feeling that Davida could only conclude that Miss Baugh had made a conquest. As they settled down to wait out the tedium of departing with so many other vehicles preceding them, Davida wondered why it was that, except for a minor pang of regret that she would not see those cherry trees in Kent, she felt no great paroxysm of pain at the thought of Hugh and Miss Baugh making a match. Reflecting on the matter for some minutes, she decided that she truly had never wanted marriage to Hugh. Nevertheless, she waited until they had left the Downs and were halfway to London before putting the inevitable question to him.

"Hugh," she enquired, "are you in love with Miss Baugh?"

Hugh flushed red as a beet. "My dear Miss Cooper," he protested, "what sort of question is that?"

"A highly impertinent one, I'm sure," Davida said in her friendliest tone. "I suspect I have been in Cassie's company much too long, for she is so used to speaking her mind freely at every turn. But the question stands, and I am determined to know the answer. Are you in love with Miss Baugh?"

Hugh had withstood Cassie's earlier assault without flinching, and he found himself now clinging to the remnants of his dignity, reminding Davida that whatever his feelings for Miss Baugh, he had made *her* an offer of marriage.

"Yes," Davida agreed, one hand holding on to her hat, which was threatening to fly off in the wind. "But that's beside the point." She smiled at him. "Do be sensible,

Hugh. If you are in love with Miss Baugh—and I suspect you are, because you give all the signs of it, particularly in your eyes which shine so much, and that, according to some, is a sure sign of love—you have only to say the word. I shall be glad to let you cry off."

"Let me cry off?" Hugh exclaimed. He turned to her with a face suffused with such gratitude that she felt momentarily piqued. There was no need for him to look *that* relieved!

Perhaps Hugh himself came to the same conclusion for he immediately rearranged his features and began to speak in the tone of one inured to misfortune: "If that is really what you wish, Miss Cooper..."

The absurdity of it all made Davida laugh. "Oh, do let us cut line and have it out," she said briskly. "I do think it wisest to marry whomever one loves, even though sometimes that is impossible. Only think of Caro Lamb and poor Lord Byron, for example. And even though I am not the least bit like her—for I never dampened my petticoats deliberately the way she did—and I do not think you so dissolute a creature as Byron, you must get my point."

Hugh, who had followed this story with some difficulty, replied that he supposed he did.

"And while we might have some affection for each other," Davida went on, "it is more in the nature of that between a brother and sister, I suspect, than anything deeper."

Hugh looked miserable as he declared, "Oh, Davida, you have been so good and kind to me. I really don't know how I could have done such a thing to you."

Davida sensibly replied that he was not to torment himself further with such thoughts. "For I am quite certain you will be twice as happy with Miss Baugh, who will make you exactly the sort of wife a diplomat should have. She is so interested in Wellington."

"Yes, I have noticed that," Hugh said. He looked sheepish and gratified at the same time as he announced to Davida that she was a regular trump.

"I suppose I am," the trump replied, "but for now you must tell me all about your Ernestine." Since this was a topic dear to his heart they were able to pass the remainder of the journey with him holding forth on Miss Baugh's many virtues. As soon as he had pulled up on the flagway at Upper Wimpole Street, Davida commanded him to go.

"There's no reason to dawdle. I'm certain you can be at the Baughs in time for afternoon tea, or with a little luck—" and here she grinned "—perhaps dinner?"

Hugh kissed her hand, announced that he would be forever in her debt, and lost no time in following this suggestion. She watched him leave with a pensive little smile, which faded when she turned and found Lyall observing her.

"You were eavesdropping!" she accused.

His eyes glinted appreciatively. "It was totally inadvertent," he confessed. "And I overheard nothing more than Hugh's undying appreciation. I own to some curiosity, Miss Cooper. You were giving him his congé, I presume, and yet he looks too suffused with gratitude for that!"

"What happened between Mr. Sylvester and myself is no concern of yours," Davida reminded him, pausing as angry voices erupted from the house.

"Cassie and her captain." Lyall answered the unspoken question in her eyes. "Having what sounds to be a devil of a quarrel."

His explanation was interrupted by Cassie's voice ringing from an upstairs window.

"The shouting is the least of it," Lyall told Davida. "Prior to that came a flurry of door slamming. Lady Aldyth says she will not worry until one of them starts hurling furniture."

Davida was aghast. "She has no right to behave like that. And why is she so angry? I thought she wasn't even speaking to the captain?"

"Words erupted on the way home," Lyall revealed, accompanying her into the house. "I was a reluctant witness to it, since my carriage was pressed into service for transport, and the syllables continued to explode in rather rude fashion long after their arrival here."

As they both stood in the hallway they could hear Cassie urging the captain to go back to his Spanish harem.

"Harem?" Lyall asked.

"For I shan't marry you," Cassie shouted. "I shan't! I shan't!"

"That suits me just fine," the captain roared back. A moment later he appeared at the top of the stairs carrying his satchel, which had now been through one more battle to add to its many scars. Quickly he brushed past Lyall and Davida and out the door.

"Someone must stop him," Davida said, and since Lyall looked unwilling to apply himself to this task, she hurried after Captain Fitzwilliam. At the sound of her voice he turned.

"You can't leave like this, Bruce," she chided as he shifted his satchel impatiently from one hand to the other.

"I'm very sorry, Davida," he said, speaking slowly and with some effort. "Pray make my excuses to your mother. But you heard Cassie yourself. Our engagement is ended."

"But she always breaks her engagement to you when she is vexed," Davida reminded him. "And you have done the same when you've fallen out of temper with her."

"That is different," he replied. "And I did not travel all this way from Spain to be made sport of."

"No, of course you didn't," Davida soothed. "But I think I know what happened. She was actually trying to help me. I know it sounds peculiar, but Hugh—Mr. Sylvester, that is—had offered for me. And Cassie thought that he was not the right person for me. I daresay she was right, because on the way home we have agreed that we wouldn't suit."

The captain impatiently remarked that while all this might be of interest to Davida and her family, it was not to him. "And I must leave now."

"But where do you plan to go at such a time?" Davida asked.

"My uncle in Gloucestershire is anxious to see me."

"No, please stay in London," Davida pleaded.

The captain squared his jaw. "Nothing could induce me to stay here."

"Not here," Davida said impatiently. "At a hotel. The Clarendon is said to be quite the best. You are tired and worried now. If you feel the same tomorrow you can depart for Gloucestershire, or you can come and visit us. I'm sure you'll feel differently. I'll try and smooth things over with Cassie."

While maintaining that he wished to make nothing smooth between himself and Cassie, the captain nonetheless agreed to remain in London. "Only because I am too fatigued for the immediate trip to Gloucestershire."

Feeling that she had won the battle if not the war, Davida wearily returned to the house, where she found her sister surrounded by Lady Aldyth, Lady Susan, and the marquis, who looked as though he wished he were anywhere but in the sitting room. Lyall hovered near the door.

"Mama, I am *not* marrying Bruce," Cassie insisted just as Davida stepped into the sitting room. "I wouldn't marry him if he were the last man on earth."

"Has the captain left?" Lyall asked Davida quietly.

She nodded. "But not forever, I hope."

"Do stop talking fustian," Lady Aldyth implored her daughter. "The way you talked to Captain Fitzwilliam, it is no surprise to me that he left. And if you continue to speak in that hoydenish fashion, he may take your threats seriously and stay away for good."

"I hope he does," Cassie replied, crossing her arms on her chest and looking as mulish as she could.

"Now, that is idiotish," Lady Aldyth said, throwing up her hands. "You have only to recall how you pined away for his letters when he was gone for only two years. Forever is much longer than that!"

"Mama is right," Davida agreed, rounding on her sister. "You have treated Bruce abominably, Cassie. I had all I could do to persuade him to remain in London."

"I don't care where he stays," Cassie said, putting up her chin. "You heard him call me a schoolroom miss. And he called me a flirt and other horrid things." Her lip trembled at the memory. "Even if he does crawl back to me I shan't take him. I intend to marry someone else."

Davida stepped back in stupefaction. "Someone else? Who else is there for you to marry except Bruce?"

"Lyall," Cassie replied. "I shall marry Lord Lyall!"

CHAPTER NINETEEN

IT WOULD HAVE BEEN impossible to say who was the most astonished by Cassie's announcement: her mother, who started noticeably at her words, her sister, who could not believe a word of it, or her prospective bridegroom, who was being rigorously interrogated by his own sister.

"Jeremy, have you been toying with this child's affections?" Lady Susan demanded.

Her brother, while acknowledging that his memory was shockingly bad, coolly maintained that he had done nothing of the sort and took temporary refuge in the sherry that John offered him, downing the glass in but one gulp.

"Of course he has not been toying with my affections," Cassie said, summoning their attention back to where she sat pouting on the couch. "It wouldn't have mattered if he had tried, for I was betrothed to Bruce and quite determined to marry him. But I'm no longer attached to odious Captain Fitzwilliam."

Davida begged her sister not to be a goose.

"I shall be a goose if I marry Bruce," Cassie insisted. "And I shan't. I'm marrying Lyall instead. You may not like him enough to think of marrying him, Davida," she said with disarming candour, "but I do. And I think we shall suit admirably."

"Kind words, Miss Cassie," Lyall drawled, keeping his hand on the decanter John had conveniently left at his elbow. "But I wonder why you did not think to inform me of all this in private, and spare me the mortification of a public disclosure.''

"Don't be exasperating, Lyall," Davida objected. "You are not mortified in the least. But I certainly am." She glared at her sister. "You are all about in your head, Cassie, to say such a preposterous thing. How do you plan on dragging Lord Lyall to the altar?"

As a younger sister, Cassie was quite accustomed to having her ideas dismissed as foolish and preposterous, and she cast a superior look at Davida now.

"I don't need to drag Lyall anywhere. I shall just enforce the marriage contract."

As the full impact of her words hit all those cognizant of the contract, the only one still ignorant of it demanded to know just what her daughters were babbling about.

"The contract Papa drew up with Lyall's father," Cassie explained to her mother. "Davida says they must have been in their cups to have done such a thing, but I don't care. I mean to enforce it."

Lady Aldyth ran her gaze despairingly from the faded Wilton to the ceiling. "The child is not making any sense," she declared.

The "child," much stung, stamped her foot. "I am telling you the truth, Mama! Just ask Davida. 'Twas she, after all, who discovered the contract, and that is how everything that has happened, happened."

Davida, acutely aware of the confusion on Lady Aldyth's face, made a vain attempt to stem the tide that seemed to be rising against her with every word Cassie uttered.

"Now do be sensible, Cassie," she chided. "You have quarrelled with Bruce and are in the hips. You know the contract is irrelevant."

"I know you never meant to enforce it yourself, Davida," Cassie said. "Nor did I in the beginning. But I have changed my mind, which is the prerogative of our sex. And the contract says either of us, being Papa's daughters, has a right to any son of Exley's, and he has only the one son, Lyall. Besides, why shouldn't I marry Lyall if I want to? I know he is not as bold and courageous as Bruce is, but since the war is no longer on, that is not such a fault."

Lady Aldyth stood, driven to the wall. "Will one of you explain this contract to me before I do murder?" she demanded.

Conscious of the lurid tale Cassie would concoct, Davida dealt her sister a quelling look and plunged into a sketchy history of the marriage contract that had been unearthed after her father's demise. Lady Aldyth heard her in stunned silence.

"I vow I had not a clue such a thing existed," she said at last. "But you should have told me this from the first, Davida."

"I know, Mama," Davida replied. "But I thought—a ridiculous notion, I'm sure—that you might actually wish the contract to be enforced, and since Cassie was practically betrothed to Bruce, that would mean I should have to marry Lyall."

"A fate worse than death itself," Lyall murmured.

Davida pretended not to hear him. "As I didn't even know Lord Lyall it seemed nothing would come of the contract. But on the other hand, I was emboldened to meet him because that might prove helpful in meeting others."

"Particularly widowers," Cassie added.

"Widowers?" Lady Aldyth's eyebrows rose.

"For you, Mama," Cassie said with a smile.

"Except that my imagination boggled at the prospect of bringing all this about," Lyall explained, stepping into the floundering conversation. "That's when I turned to Susan for help."

Lady Aldyth turned an accusatory eye on Lady Susan. "Susan, you mean you knew of this?"

"Yes, I'm afraid so," Susan admitted.

"Davida!" Lady Aldyth rounded next on her daughter. "How could you have concocted such a scheme!"

Davida had been wondering just that for the better part of a quarter hour. "I don't know, Mama. But the situation did appear urgent."

"And no one thought the opportunity to meet eligible gentlemen would be that distressing to you," Lady Susan pointed out.

"And you did meet the marquis," Lyall said, clinching the matter.

Lady Aldyth gazed over at Alwyn. "Good heavens, did you know of this too, Giles?"

"Not all of it. But I did know something was afoot the way Exley was acting. Still, you can't blame Davida for taking an interest in your affairs."

"No, but such a high-handed way of expressing an interest! However, that is all in the past," Aldyth said, washing her hands of that problem and turning to confront the current one, in the person of her younger daughter.

"Now, Cassie, do be sensible and drop your idiotish idea of marriage to Lyall."

Cassie put up her chin, more mulish than ever. "Why must I? I think he is the very husband for me. He is acknowledged to be one of the prize catches of the marriage mart. You can see for yourself that he is rather handsome, and accomplished, I am told, in sport and dress—"

"Oh, do try for a little conduct, you disgraceful child!" Davida scolded, quite aghast, as Lyall, with shoulders quaking, gazed intently the length of the room. "You are putting Mama and me to the blush with such talk. You are in love with the captain. Everyone knows that."

This, however, was the wrong thing to say. The mere mention of Captain Fitzwilliam hardened Cassie's resolve. "I certainly do not love him," she contradicted. "And I am quite within the terms of the contract to insist that Lyall marry me."

At this point Lyall himself intervened in the debate with the offhand remark that Cassie was correct, and if she so wished, a valid contract could be enforced between the two of them.

Cassie beamed. "I told you he was the very husband for me. And it's not as though I am stealing him from anyone. He's not dangling after anyone, either."

"But you can't wish to marry him," Lady Susan exclaimed as she envisioned her brother marching down some church aisle with quite the wrong bride at his side. "Oh, no, my dear Cassie. You cannot have thought it through. Marriage to Lyall would be quite detestable to you. It's not that he is *so* bad, for after all, he is my brother and possesses some modicum of address and charm, but he can be quite hardheaded when he wants his way, which is practically all the time. And he is so accustomed to ordering people about as though it were for their own good, when quite frequently it is nothing of the sort. No, my dear. It would be much wiser for you to wed your captain."

Lyall, while appreciative of his sister's efforts, would have wished that she had been a trifle less enthusiastic in detailing his flaws. But her words did not have any effect on Cassie, who insisted that Captain Fitzwilliam was no longer her captain.

"Don't be a shatterbrain, Cassie," Davida said. "Lyall doesn't wish to marry you."

"But my wishes do not matter a groat," Lyall pointed out, unperturbed. His eyes flitted briefly to Davida's face, then over to Cassie's. "But perhaps, Cassie, you might give some thought to the possibility of letting your sister claim me if she wishes. She is your elder.''

Whatever Davida had expected to hear, this certainly was not it, and she went stiff with rage, hardly hearing Cassie's response that Davida had seemed set on marrying Hugh.

''But if she does wish to marry you, I shan't stand in her way,'' Cassie offered magnanimously. ''But does she?''

''We shall have to ask her,'' Lyall said urbanely, and glanced at Davida, who was nearly speechless.

Marry Lyall to save him from a ridiculous marriage to Cassie? A pretty sort of sacrifice that would be. And an addled type of marriage. She did her best to close her ears to the voice within which quite brazenly was advising her to seize the opportunity now at hand.

''Oh, do say something,'' Lady Susan urged breathlessly. ''I vow I can't bear this suspense a moment longer.''

Obligingly Davida rose from her chair, her heart pounding and her throat dry. ''My dear Lord Lyall, I have heard you come up with outrageous and audacious, not to mention insufferable, remarks before, but they all pale when compared to this latest pearl of wisdom. Marry you? I'd liefer—''

''Drown in the Channel, or something equally ill-advised and fatal,'' Lyall said coolly. ''I do get your drift, Miss Cooper, and we needn't press you further for a response. Not,'' he added, ''that it came as any great shock to me.''

''Does that mean we shall have to wish Hugh happy?'' Lady Susan asked.

''I am not marrying Hugh,'' Davida stated firmly, settling that question once and for all. ''But I am not marrying Lyall in order to save him from Cassie's clutches.''

''Very noble of you,'' Lyall said without batting an eyelash.

"Then it's settled," Cassie said, undeterred by her sister's judgement of her motives. "I am marrying Lyall."

THE REST OF THE DAY passed with Cassie still in high gig, and Lyall, having made a rapid adjustment to his role of engaged man, taking her for a drive in the park. He was persuaded by Lady Aldyth to stay for dinner, a circumstance that greatly tasked Davida's patience, particularly since she had a perfect view of him smiling at Cassie and exchanging what appeared to be sweet nothings over their plates.

"I do wish you would tell her not to simper at him, Mama," Davida implored that night when she went in to say good-night to her mother.

Lady Aldyth had just donned a wispy dressing gown, and as she knotted the sash she eyed her daughter speculatively.

"Oh, I don't think she simpered at him, Davida. Neither of you ever adopted such mannerisms. But on the off chance that she might have picked up such a habit I shall speak with her. But perhaps," she added after another careful look at her daughter, "Lyall enjoys the simpering."

"Then he's more of a dolt than I used to think," Davida said.

"Davida!" Her mother was shocked.

Davida threw herself down on her mother's bed. "Oh, I know it is horrid of me to say such a thing, but they quite put me out of patience. Lyall doesn't love her nor she him."

"Perhaps not, but he seems genuinely fond of her."

"He is fonder of his cattle than any mere female," Davida retorted with such spirit that Lady Aldyth felt hope renew itself in her breast. She drew the dressing gown more securely about her tiny frame.

"Davida, do you wish to marry Lyall?" she inquired, sitting down on the bed next to her daughter. "For if you do, I am sure you have only to say so and Cassie—"

"I do not wish to marry Lyall," Davida said emphatically, outraged that her mother might think such a thing. "I simply don't wish to see my sister make a cake out of herself."

But in the days that followed it became obvious to Davida that Cassie had no such scruples herself. After two days spent waiting for Cassie to come to her senses and allow Captain Fitzwilliam to call on her, Davida took matters into her own hands, dispatching John to the Clarendon to request that the captain meet her at Somerset House at eleven the following morning.

With Lady Susan pressed into duty as her companion, Davida arrived at Somerset House Thursday morning to find the captain anxiously pacing by himself in a small room. He halted his stride when he caught sight of Davida, but his face fell when he noticed Susan with her instead of Cassie.

"She is at home," Davida explained as Lady Susan tactfully fell back a few steps, pretending a complete and unwarranted interest in a Greek urn.

"Does she know I'm still here in London?" the captain asked, walking on ahead with Davida.

She nodded. "Yes, I'm convinced of it. But you must know how she is by now, Bruce. She is as intractable as an ox."

"You were right, Davida," he acknowledged as she sat down on a small settee. "I have forgotten our ridiculous quarrel. All I want is the chance to see her again."

"I'm sure that can be arranged," Davida said with more conviction in her voice than in her heart, for Cassie's moods were notoriously unpredictable. "But before we go further I feel obliged to tell you that she has gotten herself engaged."

Captain Fitzwilliam had been listening to Davida respectfully and would have borne with equanimity the news that Cassie never wished to lay eyes on him again in her life, but now he gaped openly at this new and startling display of his beloved's volatility.

"Engaged, did you say?" he roared.

Conscious of the curious looks thrown their way by others in the gallery, Davida attempted to soothe him, saying the situation was not as bad as it sounded.

"Who is the scoundrel?"

"It's Lyall," she confessed with some trepidation, for the captain was looking quite fierce. "She has gotten the ridiculous notion in her head to marry him, and thus far no one has been able to talk her out of it."

"I should have known," the captain said grimly as he ran a finger around his cravat. "I shall call him out at once."

"No, you can't do that," Davida said, laying a restraining hand on his arm. "Lyall actually has nothing to do with it. And there is no real way he could get out of this engagement to Cassie." Seeing the incredulous look on the captain's face, she was obliged to explain all about the marriage contract which gave any daughter of Cutter Cooper the right to take the son of Exley as a husband.

The captain sat brooding in silence for a few minutes. Then he lifted his head. "Does Cassie love Lyall?"

"Oh, no!" she exclaimed. "You must not think such a thing, Bruce. She is just angry with you."

The captain scowled, looking unconvinced. "But she wrote to me in Spain that she was going to wed Lyall," he said gruffly.

"She did?" Davida was stupefied. "It was no doubt just one of those stupid things she was always writing to get you to return home more quickly. Quite foolish, but she has missed you enormously." She paused a moment and then impulsively invited Bruce back to Upper Wimpole Street with her. "I know that all we need do is thrust you in a room with Cassie, and she will end this ridiculous engagement to

Lyall. Unless," she suggested as the captain hesitated, "you have ceased to love her."

To her relief he flared up at once. "I shall love her forever."

"Good, then let's have no more gloom." She rose from the bench. "We shall set about ending this ridiculous quarrel between the two of you once and for all." Feeling rather pleased with this plan of action, they went off together to detach Lady Susan from her growing entanglement with Grecian urns.

Davida's certainty that Cassie would be happy to see the captain evaporated when they returned to Upper Wimpole Street and found her about to set out on a drive with Lyall. At the sight of the captain accompanying Davida and Lady Susan, Lyall drew to a stop with Cassie in the carriage.

"Good morning, Cassie," the captain said, swinging himself down from his saddle in one easy motion.

"I am sorry, Captain Fitzwilliam," Cassie said in a tone that would have sent temperatures plummeting in the desert, "so kind of you to call. But I've started on a call of my own, and we are very late, are we not, Lord Lyall?" she asked, favouring Lyall with a flirtatious smile.

"Not that late," he said dampeningly. "And I suspect the delay is inconsequential when compared to the urgency of the captain's visit. He seems to desire a word with you."

"If it's not inconvenient," the captain said stiffly.

Cassie frowned. "Oh, very well. Have you come to apologize?"

If a bolt of lightning from the summer sky had struck the captain he could not have been more rooted to the earth.

"*Apologize?* It's you who by rights should apologize to me. Leading me to believe you were engaged to Lyall against your will, and then telling me when I got here that that was nothing but a hum, and then trying to attach yourself like a leech to that fellow, Sylvester, and when I cut up stiff over that you reattach yourself to Lyall!''

"I do not think he came to apologize," Lyall murmured faintly.

Neither party to the quarrel paid him the slightest attention.

"Then why have you come?" Cassie asked darkly.

"Davida told me about your engagement," the captain said coldly. "I came to wish you happy."

Cassie paled. "Oh, you are horrid," she exclaimed. "Drive on, Lyall, do. I can't tolerate this a second longer."

Lyall correctly surmised that the attempted reconciliation had come to naught and obeyed Cassie's order. The captain stood aside as the carriage passed, looking so forlorn that Davida urged him into the house for a cup of tea.

"No, thank you," he said, rousing himself slightly. "I must return to the hotel and pack."

"Oh, Bruce!" Davida said impatiently. "You can't give up yet. What a mouse that shall make you. Cassie is just being childish. She may have spoken this way to you in public, but I'm sure that in private you can persuade her to end her engagement to Lyall."

The captain was already regretting his impetuous words to Cassie and was slightly encouraged by Davida's statement. "I would like to try again," he said.

Davida smiled. "Good. Call on us tomorrow morning. I shall make certain she sees you."

"Tomorrow," he promised, and rode off looking more cheerful.

This was more than could be said of Cassie herself, who returned two hours later to find no Captain Fitzwilliam cooling his heels in the drawing room.

"Do you mean he left?" she demanded, finding Davida all alone in the sitting room except for a bowl of fruit she was attempting to sketch.

Davida had been frowning at the peaches on her sketch pad, which in no way matched the real ones on the table, and she put down her pencil in some exasperation. She had had her fill of Cassie's whims, and oblivious to the presence of Lyall, who had followed Cassie into the room, she pointed out the many uncivil actions which had caused the unfortunate Captain Fitzwilliam to believe Cassie had no desire to talk to him.

"I don't wish to talk to him," Cassie said crossly, yanking off her hat. "I merely wished to know if he cared enough to wait and see me. Obviously, he does *not*."

"And who could possibly blame him?" Davida asked, astounded. "Such shabby treatment you've given him since he returned."

Cassie flushed and bit her lip. "But he gave me much worse, Davida. Accusing me of being on the scramble for Lyall, which I never was, and then telling me that I had set my cap at Hugh, when you and I both know that I was merely trying to prevent Hugh from marrying you." Her voice broke suddenly. "But none of that matters. Bruce doesn't love me anymore," she wailed and fled from the room in tears.

Davida, surprised by her sister's reaction, fixed the remainder of her anger on Lyall, who was standing with her sketch pad in hand, appearing not the least discomposed by witnessing such a stormy episode.

"I wonder how you can just stand there," Davida said accusingly.

He glanced up with some surprise. "My dear Miss Cooper, what would you have me do? Run after your sister and dry the tears that she is evidently shedding for some other man? My chivalrous motives stop short of that, and Wilkes tells me salt water is very hard on my coats."

"I don't care a rush about your coats," Davida said, "and give me that." She took back her sketchbook. "And you needn't act so odiously smug."

"Am I acting odiously smug? How odd. Up to now I thought I was acting just as any engaged man should at being betrothed to such a pretty young lady."

Davida, arranging her sketches in her book, felt a wholly unwarranted pang of envy. "You sound as though you want to marry Cassie."

"That might be a slight exaggeration," Lyall conceded with a chuckle. "I'm not fond of Parson's Mousetrap. But on the other hand, there is no need for me to cut up stiff over it and play the tragedy. I suppose we have you to thank for the captain's little visit?"

"Yes," Davida said, discouraged that the reconciliation had gone badly.

"One would almost think that you did not wish to see me married," Lyall said, peering at her in the most disconcerting way. "A ridiculous notion, I'm sure."

"Highly ridiculous," Davida agreed. "For my actions concern my sister, sir, and not you. It is a matter of coincidence that you and she are linked this way. My only motive is to keep her from contracting an unsuitable match with a man who in no way resembles the type of gentleman I think she should marry."

"Well, that certainly puts me in my place," Lyall said.

"And furthermore," Davida added, furious to discover that he was laughing at her, "I would not have to resort to such activities if you co-operated. You could get Cassie to break off her engagement to you."

Lyall rubbed his chin. "By playing the ugly, I suppose you mean. You may be right, but it goes against my grain to be rude and unpleasant to Miss Cassie."

"You show no such qualms, however, about being rude and unpleasant to me," she pointed out.

He smiled appreciatively. "But you are not Cassie. And if it's a broken engagement you desire, you could have accomplished that earlier."

"Only by sacrificing myself," Davida retorted.

Lyall blinked. "Too harsh, Miss Cooper. I own that marriage to me might entail minor inconveniences, but hardly a mortal sacrifice. Or perhaps you fancy yourself one of those tropical maidens who find their way into the nearest volcano!"

"Of course I am no such thing!" Davida shot back.

"Well, I am relieved," Lyall said sympathetically. "And perhaps you have forgotten that I have a considerable fortune. That ought to attract you."

"Your fortune is of no interest to me."

"Nor was Hugh's now that I think of it," Lyall said. "And I am on pins and needles to hear how that story came to an end. I saw him in the park this morning with Miss Baugh. Such looks of devotion that they exchanged. I told Cassie we must contrive to imitate those soulful expressions. Miss Baugh, I take it, cut you out with Hugh?"

Davida, stung by this bare-bones description of a situation that was infinitely more complicated than that, answered that she had declined Hugh's offer for private reasons.

"Hmm." Lyall was sceptical. "I hope you don't wear the willow for him, for that would be a complete waste. Miss Baugh has dazzled him silly. It's rather hard to compete with a Wellington enthusiast. But I'm certain a woman of your charms can find another soul mate. Perhaps I can help you. I did rather well with your mother."

"Thank you," Davida said stiffly. "But I can find my own soul mate without your assistance. And you would do better to find one of your own."

"But I have found one," Lyall replied blithely. "Haven't I?"

CHAPTER TWENTY

SOUL MATES, INDEED, Davida fumed to herself that evening as she entered the Baughs' drawing room for a small rout party. No one, however, seeing her in the soft turquoise satin gown she had chosen to wear, would have had a clue that she could just as easily have strangled her sister as look at her. And even looking at her was a penance, for it entailed the view of Cassie clinging like a wraith to Lyall's arm.

"As though you had the consumption," Davida informed her at the first opportunity.

Cassie, who was looking quite gay in apple-green cambric, replied with a saucy bounce of her curls that she saw nothing amiss in her behaviour, nor did Lyall.

"Which only proves the worst of my suspicions!" Davida retorted. But she was bound to admit, as her gaze drifted over to Lyall—thick in conversation with Lady Susan and Lady Baugh—that he at least was attempting to behave with some appearance of good conduct, and that it was Cassie who was throwing caution to the wind as well as every notion of gentility instilled in her at great cost by their numerous governesses.

A chance remark that Cassie let fall indicating her belief that Bruce would be joining the party gave Davida an inkling as to her sister's motives.

"Bruce is not attending."

Cassie's eyes narrowed. "Why not?" she demanded.

"I have no idea," Davida replied. "Miss Baugh told me he sent his regrets. So I do hope you realize that your act of complete devotion to Lyall is unnecessary and utterly wasted on the rest of us."

"What makes you think it is an act?" a voice quizzed, and Davida turned to be confronted by Lyall himself.

"Must you always eavesdrop?" she asked sharply, impatient with him for appearing out of nowhere and impatient with herself for the stupid way her heart leapt at the sound of his voice.

"Indeed not," he said in answer to her complaint. "But it does strike me that you always seem to be accusing me of eavesdropping, so perhaps in my own defence I ought to take it up. Nothing is more annoying than to be accused continually of a crime one has not committed."

Annoyed at the way he twisted her innocent remark, Davida was about to launch into a pungent recitation of the various habits he would do better to pursue than eavesdropping, when Hugh arrived.

He greeted them all with a friendly smile, but Davida would have had to be blind if she had failed to notice how he searched the room for Miss Baugh and sped off to her side.

"If that's not love," Lyall remarked in her ear, "I wish to know what is."

"Your theories on love do not concern me in the least, Lyall," Davida said brusquely as she moved away.

She stood by herself for a moment, witnessing out of the corner of one eye the pleasantries going on between Hugh and Miss Baugh. The sight gave rise to the most conflicting emotions. On the one hand, she had never been in love with Hugh; on the other hand, it was certainly agreeable to be courted by a gentleman like him. And while she had no real claim to his volatile affections, she did think a truer gentleman would have arranged to show less obvious delight in Miss Baugh's company.

Lady Baugh, trailing mauve draperies that made her look more nervous than ever, fluttered up just then to shoo them into the dining room. There Davida listened with every appearance of fascination to Sir Edwin Baugh's plan to eventually raise Arabians on his estate, which now boasted nothing but the most deplorably short-boned creatures.

When dinner was over, everyone went into the Green Saloon to hear Miss Baugh on the harp. After that, Davida found herself involved in a game of whist with Lyall, of all people, as her partner.

"Surely Cassie..." she said as he held out a chair for her.

"Your sister has not inherited your mother's affinity for cards," Lyall observed, "which I as her prospective husband can only applaud."

"Then perhaps Mr. Sylvester."

"I think Hugh is partnering Miss Baugh on the terrace. You'll find me a tolerable partner, Miss Cooper."

At this Lady Susan, who was already seated and fiddling impatiently with the cards, adjured her brother to stop being so modest. "It ill becomes you."

"I beg pardon, Sue," he said smoothly, "and I shall try not to be so humble."

While Davida could not discern any change in his humility, she was bound to admit that he played well. His bidding was shrewd, and he handled his cards with skill if not with the great and fleeting brilliance that characterized Sir Edwin's game. Her own play in the match was erratic, due in large measure to finding Lyall's eyes on her quite often during the course of the game.

"You play well," he said an hour later when the game had ended. "But you might have played better if you had concentrated on your cards."

"I might have played better," she agreed, "if you had not been staring at me in that horridly rude fashion."

He looked amused. "What an absurd creature you are. I was not staring at you at all."

"What do you call it, then?" she asked, lifting her chin.

He smiled. "If I were of a more poetic frame of mind I might say I was lost in admiration of you!"

"Admiration," she scoffed. "That's Spanish coin, Lyall. You don't admire me in the least. You think me high-handed and managing—"

"You woefully underestimate yourself, Miss Cooper." He shook his head. "And you malign me!"

"Davida!" Hugh suddenly broke in between them, leading Miss Baugh by the hand. They were grinning from ear to ear. "You don't mind, I hope, Jeremy," he added.

Lyall took a step back. "Not at all, Hugh," he said. "I have always preferred having my Hessians trampled, particularly when I am still wearing them."

Hugh paid no heed to his friend's complaint, and informed them that while they had been involved in cards, he had offered for Miss Baugh and been accepted.

"How wonderful!" Davida exclaimed. "I do wish you happy."

Lyall forgot about his boots and echoed her sentiments.

"Thank you," Hugh said, looking pleased with himself. "But really, Davida, it was all your doing."

"Mine?"

"That talk you gave me," he explained, seeing her puzzlement. "About following my heart and never marrying except for love." He glanced sheepishly over at Miss Baugh. "It was the best advice I could have received."

Conscious of Lyall at her elbow, Davida coloured, but replied that she was glad to have helped.

"Yes," Lyall agreed. "Miss Cooper is a font of wisdom on matters of romance. In fact, she shows a marked affinity for playing Cupid. I first noticed this talent myself a fortnight ago."

Hugh, however, cut short Lyall's story, asking to be excused and explaining that they must tell the others the good news. He swept off with Miss Baugh giddily hanging on his every word.

Unfortunately, Davida thought, Hugh did not sweep Lyall along with him, for he remained at her side, once again examining his Hessians with his quizzing glass.

"Is the damage that severe?" Davida inquired.

"Not to my eye or yours," he replied. "But valets are blessed with second sight. And I shall no doubt be in Wilkes's black books." Resigning himself to this inevitable fate, he dropped the quizzing glass and abruptly turned the topic. "Did you actually tell Hugh to follow his heart?"

Davida's eyes had been diverted to his boots, and she now jerked her head up, coolly replying that that was none of his concern.

His lips curved in a smile. "You don't know how wrong you are."

"Very well, then. If you must know, yes. I told Hugh to marry whomever he loved, a notion you would never agree with."

"On the contrary," he said quite calmly. "I subscribe to that idea wholeheartedly. I have always wished to marry for love, if," he added, "I married at all. But my wishes seem to be of no consequence in my marriage to come." He paused and dipped into his pocket for his snuffbox. "Do you think in time Cassie will grow to love me?"

"I neither know nor care, sir," Davida said politely.

His brow lifted. "She is your sister," he pointed out.

"Yes, and unfortunately she seems determined to marry you. Whenever your marriage comes to pass, that shall be your doing and hers, not mine."

An odd glint showed momentarily in Lyall's eyes. "Yes, but I have the strangest suspicion that until our wedding day does arrive you will move heaven and earth to prevent Cassie from marrying me."

His comment was so near the mark that Davida turned wildly and stalked off, blind to where she might be going. Fortunately, Lady Baugh headed her off when she was halfway across the room, bubbling over with the good news of her daughter's betrothal, and Davida was able to felicitate her with every expression of goodwill. Then she moved on to join her mother, who had been in conversation with Lady Susan.

"I must say your brother is acting the part of the devoted suitor to perfection," Davida commented to Lady Susan.

Susan was startled to find Davida next to her. "What did you say, my dear?"

"Just that Lyall is a greater actor than Mr. Kean!"

"I wonder if he is playing a part," Susan mused. "You may think it odd and I vow, so do I in a way, but I have heard him say at least a dozen times that when the time was right to marry, he'd look to the schoolroom."

Davida burst out laughing. "That may be true, but I can hardly imagine Cassie can be confused with the sort of schoolroom miss your brother had in mind."

Lady Susan laughed, along with Aldyth, and went on, "But he might be the very man to make a match of Cassie."

"Susan, do you mean you approve of the match?" Lady Aldyth asked.

"Scarcely days ago you were as opposed to it as we were!" Davida added.

"I have been giving the matter considerable thought," Lady Susan told them. "While Cassie might not be the bride I had foreseen for him, she does stand on excellent terms with him. And there have been more improbable matches in the ton—take the Regent's, for example. So perhaps Lyall's marriage to Cassie will not be so horrendous after all.''

''It will be a nightmare,'' Davida declared. ''He has no interest in her whatsoever. Until she broached the idea, he had never given her a moment's thought.''

''True, but she did bring it up, and he has been giving her considerably more than a moment's thought,'' Susan said gently as she moved away.

Susan's words remained with Davida as she retired that night. But no, it wasn't possible that Lyall could love Cassie. Whatever came to pass, she promised herself, drawing the coverlet up to her chin and thinking hard, Cassie must never marry a *detestable* man like Lyall!

THE NEXT MORNING Davida awoke with a slight headache, which she blamed on her latest quarrel with Lyall. Remembering suddenly that Captain Fitzwilliam was due to call on Cassie that morning, she felt more cheerful, dressed quickly in a lime-green frock, and descended the stairs. She found the breakfast room empty. Then she remembered Lady Aldyth had mentioned making some visits in the country with Alwyn.

''Is Cassie up?'' she asked Millie, the maid, when she came with her breakfast.

''She went out for a drive with Lord Lyall. Something about abbey ruins, I believe, Miss Davida.''

Davida frowned. She certainly hoped that Cassie would return from the abbey in time to see the captain, and that for once Lyall would be sensible and leave the two together to mend matters.

Davida finished her breakfast, then tried to do a little sketching in the sitting room. She sat by the window so that she would be able to see Cassie when she returned. Why, she wondered despairingly, had her sister chosen this morning to view the abbey ruins?

Fifteen minutes of mounting vexation passed. Finally, she heard noises on the flagway and, uttering a brief thankful ejaculation, she went to the door. But it was the captain who reined in, looking handsome and anxious and more youthful without his moustache.

"I shaved it off," he explained unnecessarily, for there was no other way it could have removed itself from his lip. "Cassie?" he asked anxiously.

"She isn't in at the moment," Davida replied.

His features turned to stone. "I see."

"No, you don't," she said irritably. "She rose early and went off on a morning ride with Lyall. She had no notion that you would be coming here. I thought it best not to tell her in case she would bolt."

"Despite those precautions she seems to have bolted just the same," the captain answered. "When do you expect her?"

"At any moment," Davida assured him. "Come and have some tea."

A half hour passed. Davida continued sketching, but found it difficult to concentrate with the captain starting at every passing sound.

"It's no use," he said finally, glaring at the clock, which showed the hour well past eleven. "It's obvious that Cassie doesn't wish to see me ever again."

Davida stifled her own exasperation. "She doesn't even know you're here," she pointed out. "If she did she would be here in a trice."

The captain shot her a look that said eloquently enough that he would believe that when he saw it himself.

"It's quite true," Davida declared. "Yesterday when Cassie returned with Lyall she was most displeased to find you gone."

The captain's face turned dark. "Displeased? Do you mean she had the gall to expect me to stay here while she and Lyall went off together?"

"Yes, she did." Davida cut short his tirade. "It is so typical of her, Bruce. No one could fault you for disliking such shabby treatment. But it shows that she's so young, headstrong, and impetuous."

"I know. She's been that way since she was a child." Bruce reflected a moment. "That's what drew me to her in the first place." He glanced at Davida. "I've made up my mind. When I see her next I don't care if Lyall's with her, I'm going to drag her away for a private chat."

As this was precisely the course she wished him to pursue, Davida bestowed a look of utter approval on him.

"That sounds like a splendid idea."

Splendid or not, the captain's plan was in abeyance since Cassie had not returned. After another quarter hour had passed Davida grew worried. The abbey was not that far away, but either rider might have taken a nasty spill. Visions of broken bones spun in her mind. She was still contemplating this dire possibility when Lady Susan was announced. She came into the sitting room in a rush, her hair askew, looking far from her usual composed self.

"Susan?"

"Oh, Davida, pray forgive me for just descending on you like this, but I had no notion where else to go."

"What is it?" Davida asked her friend. "It's not Walter, I hope. Or your daughter, Priscilla?"

Lady Susan dismissed both husband and daughter with a wave of a hand that was holding a cream-coloured paper.

"I went to call on Lyall today to try and speak to him about this marriage to Cassie. And I found this waiting for me. It's addressed to me as you can see. I came here the instant I finished reading it."

"What does it say?"

"That dreadful brother of mine has eloped with Cassie!" Lady Susan said by way of an answer.

CHAPTER TWENTY-ONE

IF LADY SUSAN HAD suddenly announced her intention of joining the nearest gypsy caravan, forsaking husband and daughter in the bargain, Davida could not have been more astonished; but her reaction was nothing when compared to that of the captain, who literally exploded from his chair at the very mention of the word *elopement* coupled in the same breath with his beloved Cassie.

"You can read the letter yourself," Lady Susan said—quite unnecessarily, for Davida had already snatched it up. With the captain leaning against her shoulder she scanned its contents.

> Dear Susan,
> No time to explain. I'm to Bath with Cassie. Say nothing and I shall be indebted to you forever.
>
> J.

"To Bath?" Davida dropped into the chair the captain had just vacated. There was no need for her to remind herself how she had provoked Lyall the night before, as good as challenging him to marry Cassie over her opposition. This, if you please, was the result.

"Is this Lyall's handwriting?" the captain was demanding of Lady Susan, who scrutinized the note again and replied that it had much the look of her brother's hand.

"Elopement," Davida murmured to herself in disbelief. She rose to her feet. "There must be some mistake. Not an elopement. And why to Bath of all places?"

"No," the captain agreed. "Not an elopement, but an abduction."

"That amounts to the same thing," Davida said crossly, impatient at such hairsplitting at a time like this. "Lyall has abducted Cassie in order to marry her. I should have known when we came to dagger points last night that something like this might happen, but truly I never did imagine. What an abominable creature!" She paced wildly for a moment. "He knew I was set against their marrying. That's why he resorted to this!"

"If marriage is indeed what he has in mind," the captain said, looking grim.

His words brought Davida to a halt. "But surely it is marriage," she said, taking only a moment to reflect on the alternative. "You cannot believe Lyall would ruin her? Good heavens, not even Lyall would stoop to such villainy."

"There are some men," replied the captain, "who would not scruple to take advantage of an innocent like Cassie."

"Yes, scoundrels to be sure," Davida agreed, resuming her pacing. "And while Lyall is not a saint and possesses far too many flaws to be at all agreeable, he is not a blackguard."

The captain demanded to know if she was defending the man who had just abducted her sister.

"Good heavens, no. Why do we spar, Captain? We must stop them at once." She turned as she spoke, nearly tripping over Lady Susan who had been following her as she paced from one end of the room to the other.

"John, I must speak to John."

A short interview with this faithful servant elicited the information that Lyall had called for Miss Cassie for the supposed trip to the abbey ruins not more than an hour and a half ago.

"I might catch up with them if I knew where they would stop en route!" the captain said after John had gone back to his duties.

"The White Castle in Falfield," Lady Susan answered promptly. As Davida shot her a quizzical glance she explained that Lyall always stopped there on his way to Bath. "To exchange horses. He vows no other hand shall touch his precious cattle."

"You are certain?" The captain pounced quickly on this first stroke of good luck.

Lady Susan nodded.

Captain Fitzwilliam rubbed his hands together. "I shall catch up to him in Falfield, and when I do I shall make him rue the day he ever contemplated such an infamous act."

"And I shall make him doubly sorry," Davida added.

The captain stared at her. "But you can't come with me, Davida," he protested, not in the least pleased to have his rescue obstructed by the company of a lady who might fall into hysteria or the vapours or the other things females were wont to do during a crisis.

"Cassie is my sister," Davida retorted, "and I don't intend to wait here wringing my hands or whatever it is that people who wait are inclined to do. Let's not argue further, Bruce. Time is flying. Susan, I see you have your carriage with you, can we induce you to lend it to us?"

"Yes, of course!" Lady Susan declared.

"Good, I shall just leave a message for Mama—" She paused, directing an agonized look at Lady Susan. "Good heavens, *Mama*! What shall I say?"

"Nothing, for the moment," Susan said firmly. "We may yet find Cassie and bring this adventure to an end."

"*We?*" the captain asked with a frown.

"Yes," Lady Susan said, pulling on her gloves. "I am coming with you." As the captain began to protest, she added that the carriage after all was hers, and Lyall was her brother.

"And that," the captain complained bitterly when the three of them were finally squeezed into the carriage, "is hardly a matter I should choose to boast about."

"I am quite sure that Jeremy has a reasonable explanation for his behaviour," Lady Susan replied.

The captain, who was driving at a wholly abandoned speed on the road to Bath, replied that the reason for Lyall's behaviour was plain enough—seduction of a young girl— and that his lordship, brother or no brother, was an out-and-out scoundrel.

Lady Susan rarely championed her brother's cause, but she felt duty-bound to defend him now as best she could. She pointed out that Cassie might have had something to do with the elopement.

"Are you implying that Cassie lured Lyall away, ma'am?" the captain asked, turning his attention from the road just as another carriage shot around the bend.

Davida's earsplitting shriek alerted the captain to the imminent danger, and muttering an oath against women who could not leave well enough alone, he managed to turn the carriage toward the wider part of the road with only an inch to spare.

While Davida let out the breath she had been holding, Lady Susan cautioned the captain on the importance of keeping his eyes on the road. She didn't relish having to explain to Walter what had happened to his vehicle!

"I am well acquainted with how to drive," Captain Fitzwilliam said, affronted by this aspersion on his driving skills. "In fact," he added as he glared at his companions, "I am acknowledged to be a first-rate whip."

"Yes, I'm sure you are," Davida said, attempting to smooth his much-ruffled feathers. "But if you would deign to look at the road now and then, it might ease my mind. I have been thinking," she added as he grudgingly complied with this last request, "that Susan is right, and Cassie may very well have to shoulder some of the blame for this escapade. You do see that this is exactly the type of romantic nonsense she would dream up, don't you? She fairly devours a score of library romances a week. Moreover, she knew how adamantly opposed we were to her marriage to Lyall. How I wish I had never discovered that wretched contract!"

Lady Susan patted her reassuringly. "You cannot blame yourself, Davida. The main thing is to stop them before the irrevocable deed is done."

Interpreting this as a command to drive like the devil, the captain increased his already breakneck speed, causing more than one irate coachman encountered on the way to Falfield to emit the vilest of oaths skyward concerning those unfit to hold a whip.

Davida was too busy berating her own stupid behaviour at the Baughs' to pay much attention to the coachmen. Nothing, she saw clearly now, could have been more fatal than to flaunt her opposition to Lyall in his face. He had taken the first opportunity to set off and marry Cassie, which only proved, Davida thought with the most peculiar pang in her heart, that his feelings for her sister ran much deeper than anyone had suspected.

In this fashion the miles flew by. It was late afternoon when they finally reached Falfield. The captain drew up into the stable yard at the White Castle, flung down the reins, and demanded of the nearest ostler if a gentleman accompanied by a young lady had passed through earlier that afternoon.

The ostler scratched his head and gawked at the sight of the three of them. "A gentleman, you say?"

"About thirty," the captain said impatiently. "Tall, well dressed."

"With a lady?" the ostler inquired, continuing to scratch his head.

"More of a girl," Lady Susan answered, having by this time climbed down from the carriage with Davida.

The ostler nodded his head. "Right enough, I have seen them."

"Which way did they go?" Lady Susan and Davida cried out together.

"When did they leave?" the captain asked, trying to regain control of the inquisition he had begun and looking as though for two pins he would throttle the ostler or the ladies on either side of him.

"Didn't," the ostler replied, stroking the horses.

"Didn't what?" the captain shouted in frustration.

"Didn't leave," the ostler said, appearing surprised at this display of emotion. He jerked a thumb toward the inn. "They're inside now, and like to turn it upside and down. Nobbin, that's the landlord, doesn't like it above half."

The captain had no interest in the likes of any landlord and had already started toward the inn with Davida and Lady Susan hot on his heels. The three entered the establishment just as a penetrating voice emanated from an upstairs floor.

"Where are they?" it roared out.

Davida's heart jumped. "That's Lyall," she cried.

With his prey at hand the captain took the stairs two at a time, while Davida, mindful of the possibility of bloodshed, followed anxiously. Lady Susan hung back, slightly out of breath.

At the top of the stairs Davida paused and caught sight of Lyall, Cassie, and a much-harried man who was apparently

Nobbin, all attempting to gain entrance to a chamber down the hall. At least Lyall and Cassie were attempting to gain entrance. The landlord was trying to prevent them from going in.

"Please, my lord," he begged, looking frantic, "the people you are searching for are not here. I have a French count in that room sleeping."

"I don't care if you have a dozen counts," Lyall responded acidly, "Russian and German in addition to French."

"Good afternoon, Lord Lyall," the captain spoke softly.

Hearing his name, Lyall turned with a frown. An oath sprang to his lips.

"So here you are, Captain Fitzwilliam," he said, his teeth flashing in a smile. "And I see Miss Cooper is right beside you."

"Did you ever doubt it?" the captain asked, advancing wrathfully to stand an arm's length from Lyall.

Before Lyall could answer, Cassie flung herself at the captain, shrieking his name in a quite besotted way.

"If you have hurt her," the captain threatened as he tightened his hold on Cassie, "I shall demand satisfaction of you, Lyall."

Cassie drew away, looking bewildered. "Hurt me? Good gracious, Bruce, what are you talking about?"

Lyall's eyes raked the captain from head to toe. "Don't be a curst fool, Fitzwilliam. It's I who shall have the pleasure of cutting you to ribbons. Unless you'd prefer pistols."

"Oh, pray, not a duel," Davida implored, speaking for the first time. "It's all your fault, you disgraceful girl," she spoke to Cassie, "running off with Lyall as though you had no notion of proper conduct!"

Cassie appeared staggered by this accusation. "*I* run off with *Lyall*?" she ejaculated. "Do be serious, Davida. I've never heard of a more idiotish notion in my life."

Davida gaped at her, unable to believe her ears. "Then you aren't eloping?" she asked. "You can't be married already, I hope!"

"Good Jupiter, no," Cassie answered, unaware of the giddy rush of relief her words sparked within her sister.

"But if you weren't eloping why did you run off with him?" the captain asked.

"Actually he wanted to go alone," Cassie confessed, "but I insisted on coming along to find you and prevent you from eloping with Davida."

This bombshell had the effect of silencing both the captain and Davida. The latter wondered if her sister had lost all her wits in the time it had taken her to journey to Falfield.

"Why would *I* elope with Bruce?" she asked when she could finally speak.

"Well, I certainly do not know," Cassie assured her. "And I own I have been puzzled, for you never showed him the slightest *tendre* during the years we've both known him."

Lyall shifted his impatient gaze from face to face and finally selected the captain as the one who could provide the most lucid answer to the day's madness.

"Were you or weren't you eloping with Miss Cooper?" he demanded.

The captain recoiled visibly. "I am not in the habit of eloping with women the way you might be, my lord. And what sort of man do you think I am?"

"The sort," Lyall answered promptly, "who would not scruple to elope with one woman and make love to her sister the minute the cheat was discovered."

The captain's face flamed. "You're bosky. And," he added, playing his ace, "how could I elope with Miss Cooper when your sister was sitting attendance on us in the carriage?"

This remark caught Lyall completely off guard. Abruptly he wheeled round and out of the sea of faces ranged along the stairs and corridor he recognized Lady Susan's.

"I think," he said in a voice that boded ill for that lady, "I must have a little chat with Susan."

Lady Susan smiled at him. "Yes, of course, Lyall. But do find us a private parlour, for we can't have a family discussion on the stairs."

Lyall thought it a bit late for such scruples, but he made arrangements for the parlour, and as soon as the door closed he turned a withering eye on his sister.

"Well, Susan? What is the meaning of this charade?"

Lady Susan believed that the best defence at the moment was an offence and responded acidly that she thought the meaning apparent to even a five-year-old child.

"You admit writing this note to me?" Lyall asked, showing her a piece of paper.

Lady Susan did not bother to glance at it. "Of course, I wrote it," she said with considerable hauteur on her face.

Observing the puzzlement on Davida's, Lyall passed her the note and gazed at his unrepentant sister. Davida scanned the note quickly, then said in astonishment, "This says I'm eloping to Falfield with Captain Fitzwilliam."

The captain, who had been availing himself of the claret provided by Nobbin, now spluttered half the glassful down his shirt. Ignoring Cassie's attempts to dry it with her handkerchief, he reached across to snatch the offending document from Davida.

"This is preposterous," he fumed.

"More than that!" Davida exclaimed. "And I for one am shocked and appalled."

"Yes, I daresay you are," was Lady Susan's calm reply.

"How did you get this?" the captain asked Lyall.

"Hugh came riding up with it when I was out driving with Cassie this morning." He gave his sister another punctilious look. "You put him up to it, of course?"

Lady Susan nodded.

"And I suppose this note you say you discovered at Lyall's residence telling us he had eloped with Cassie was a sham as well?" the captain demanded.

Lady Susan, driven to the wall by these questions, flung up her hands. "Yes! Yes!" she cried out. "It was a simple deception and there is no need for the pair of you to carry on so thunderously."

"You lied to us, Lady Susan," the captain said.

Lady Susan shifted uncomfortably under his gaze and replied that she had done no such thing. "I told you I found the note at Lyall's, which is true. Of course I placed it there myself! And I also said the writing had a great look of Jeremy's, which is also true for we do have a similar hand."

This analysis of handwriting was dismissed by everyone in the parlour except Lyall, who appeared amused.

"You misled me," Davida said to Lady Susan.

"I rather think," Lyall murmured from his chair, "that we were all misled."

"Of course I misled you," Lady Susan replied. "How else could I get the four of you together? Good heavens, Jeremy, if you could only see the situation growing more absurd with each hour! And none of you showing the slightest inclination to end it. Young Cassie here seemed so taken with you I shouldn't have wondered if she had married you just to spite all who begged her not to. And," she continued, "you were showing such dogged devotion to her that anyone would think you were serious about marrying her. Clearly someone had to take a hand in things or you'd make mice feet of it."

Lyall chuckled. "My dear Susan, your powers amaze me."

"And yours amaze me. Anyone with half your address would have extricated himself long ago from your engagement to Cassie. But instead you chose to revel in it."

Lyall sighed and stretched out his legs in front of his chair. "I do own I was getting fond of the prospect of being a married man," he said, blandly meeting his sister's incredulous stare. "Shoes by the fire, apron strings and all that," he said helpfully.

"*Fond* you may be of the prospect," the captain said with a frown, "but you won't be tied to Cassie's apron strings. She's not marrying you."

Lyall looked up almost absentmindedly. "Oh, she isn't?"

The captain fixed a baleful eye on Cassie. "Tell him so immediately, Cassie."

But now that she was once again the focus of all attention, Cassie chose to be obstinate. "I don't see why I shouldn't marry Lyall if I so wish," she persisted. Ignoring her sister's plea to stop being a ninnyhammer, she glanced from the captain to Lyall. "You could fight a duel for my hand," she said eagerly. "I've never had a duel fought over me before, and if you promise not to wound each other too severely I could be persuaded to permit you to hold it."

Lyall could not contain his laughter. "Thank you," he said, gasping for breath. "But I hope you shan't mind if I decline so enchanting a prospect."

"I don't see why you're so amused," Cassie said, her hands on her hips. "Unless you are afraid of Bruce, which I don't think you are because you have been called out before."

"Only in his salad days," Lady Susan reminded them all.

"And," Cassie went on, "you seemed quite willing to fight a duel on the way to Falfield. Even eager."

Lyall poured himself some claret and held up the glass to the sunlight. "That was different. In point of fact it would have been the captain who would be duelling over you. I would have been fighting over someone else entirely." His eyes slid over to where Davida sat.

"Do stop all this stupid talk of duels," Davida said hastily to hide the confusion she was feeling. "Cassie, you know you love Bruce, so stop being a goosecap."

"But Davida—"

"Captain Fitzwilliam," Lyall requested, "if you would heed some advice from one only recently engaged to your betrothed, I would suggest that you kiss her at once. Immediately," he emphasized.

The captain thought this the best idea he had heard all day, and Cassie emerged dishevelled but smiling from his embrace, withdrawing her claim to Lyall and accepting the captain's offer.

"Although," she said with genuine regret, "it would have been famous to have a duel fought over me."

"Yes," Lyall sympathized. "But what if, quite by accident, I grant you, I had managed to wound your captain?"

This aspect of the situation caused Cassie to cling even harder to Bruce and to assure everyone her interest in duels was on the wane.

"That's a good girl," the captain said, kissing her.

Davida stood up. "Now that that's settled, the only thing that remains is to find some way of convincing Mama that nothing has occurred, when we return to London."

"I don't think you need worry about that, Davida," a voice rang out, and into the parlour walked Lady Aldyth herself.

CHAPTER TWENTY-TWO

LADY ALDYTH'S ENTRANCE into the parlour was marked by considerable confusion, especially since she was accompanied by Alwyn and a beak-nosed man whom the marquis introduced as Reverend Bell.

"A reverend? Do you mean a minister, sir?" Cassie exclaimed. "But what is a minister doing here?"

Her question had been addressed to the marquis, but he, like Lyall and the captain, had allowed himself to become distracted by the claret on the table, and it was Lady Aldyth who finally answered that ministers generally were required when a wedding had to be performed.

Davida frowned. "But Mama, no one is getting married here," she declared, and then fell abruptly silent as the possibility struck her that Lady Aldyth, in an excess of maternal concern, had hit upon a swift wedding between Lyall and Cassie as the only solution to the possible harm inflicted on Cassie's reputation.

"Mama," she said, conscious of the need to speak discreetly in front of the august Reverend Bell, "there has been nothing amiss in the day's activities, I do assure you. All is well," she hinted, "between Cassie and Lyall, I mean."

"Miss Cooper is attempting to say that I didn't ruin Miss Cassie," Lyall spoke loudly across the table of claret, uncowed by the presence of the minister and amused by the novelty of Davida's coming to his defence.

Lady Aldyth recoiled. "Of course I know that Lyall didn't ruin Cassie."

"Then why all this talk of weddings?" Davida asked, more perplexed than ever.

The marquis laughed. "It is your mama and I who plan on getting married today, my dear Davida," he announced.

"Mama," Cassie breathed. "Are you eloping with the marquis?"

Lady Aldyth, looking quite dreamy eyed in yellow gauze, smiled at her daughter and replied that she supposed she was at that.

The marquis winked and dropped a kiss on Aldyth's cheek. "Of course we are eloping. The more I thought of a fancy wedding the more I disliked the idea. Aldyth agreed. So we hit on this. And since she had a notion there might be more than one wedding in the making I fixed these up as well. Special licences," he explained, spreading these prized documents on the table.

Davida had never seen a special licence before, and she picked one up. "But there are three here, sir," she said, looking puzzled. "Why so many?"

"One for me," Aldyth answered, "one for Cassie, and one for you."

All colour drained from Davida's face at her mother's words. She dropped the licence as though it were a burning ember.

"Really, Mama, you go too far. And I should like to know how you did manage to cross our path here." Her suspicious gaze darted from face to face. "This elopement is nothing but a hoax! You and the marquis are both part of this wild-goose chase of Lady Susan's."

There was no denying the guilt that was writ plainly on the faces of all those involved, but Lady Aldyth, fluttering a little, did her best to stem her daughter's display of emotion.

"Perhaps we did know something of it," she admitted nervously. "And I do hope you have not been blaming Lady Susan too harshly, for all of us had a hand in dreaming up the scheme. Although the idea originated with her. So clever of her, I thought!"

"But it was you, Aldyth, who hit on using Hugh to relay the message to Cassie and Lyall at the abbey, while I stayed behind to bring Davida and the captain here to Falfield," Susan said, unwilling to take all the credit for her plan.

"Mama, how could you have done such a thing!" Davida chided, her cheeks flaming red from all that she had heard.

"Well, we had to do something, my dear," Aldyth replied calmly. "We were all at sixes and sevens. And I hardly think my scheme any more outrageous than yours involving widowers," she said.

"That was different," Davida said.

"I don't see how you can say that," Lady Aldyth countered mildly. "And I did think if you and Cassie showed no scruples in taking a hand in my future, I should have none in seeing to yours. Fortunately—" she bestowed a fond smile on Cassie and Bruce "—Cassie has always, from the cradle, planned on marrying Bruce so I had no compunction getting involved there. I knew once the rumour of an elopement involving him with some other lady reached her, Cassie's true feelings would come out."

Cassie demanded to know why the other lady had been Davida.

"Miss Baugh was my first choice," Lady Susan explained, taking a glass of claret from her brother. "But she is engaged to Hugh now, and he cut up stiff over the idea. So we hit on Davida, thinking that she would not mind greatly, especially since it was for a good cause."

"Well, Davida did mind," answered that lady now, looking far from mollified by these explanations. "She minded a good deal as a matter of fact. To embroil anyone in such a scheme is quite reprehensible, abominable—''

"Not to mention insufferable," Lyall added helpfully.

He had moved to her side without anyone noticing, and she recoiled at finding him so near at hand. "I am quite capable of finding my own words, my lord," she said acidly.

Lady Aldyth, correctly deducing from this brief exchange that all was by no means settled in that part of the parlour, glanced over belatedly at Lady Susan. "Didn't we give you enough time, Susan?" she asked.

Lady Susan shook her head. "We have only this minute got Jeremy unbetrothed to Cassie and Cassie finally consenting to accept Bruce, and have not made the least progress with Davida."

"I knew we should have stopped for a bite to eat," Lady Aldyth said fretfully at the same time that her daughter demanded to know what Lady Susan was alluding to by progress with her.

"Oh, just this and that," Lady Aldyth replied, fluttering to her friend's rescue. "Shall we just say, my dear Davida, that all of us in this room have a real wish to see you happy." She punctuated this statement with a glance at Lyall.

As the meaning of her mother's words sank in, Davida nearly choked on her rage. "Mama," she threatened, "if you think for one minute—''

Her words, however, were cut short by Lyall himself, who remarked in an offhand way that there was no necessity for them to concern themselves over Miss Cooper's future.

"All is arranged," he said blithely, ignoring Davida's thundercloud look.

Lady Aldyth shrieked with joy and hugged her elder daughter to her bosom. "Lord Lyall, do you mean?"

"What are you talking about?" Davida asked, breaking loose from her mother's untimely embrace and advancing on Lyall like a wounded tigress. "Nothing whatsoever has been arranged about my future."

His eyes met hers. "Oh no? Do you mean that you have changed your mind and don't wish to be a governess after all? I wish you had said something beforehand," he complained, "for I had the perfect household selected for you. Sir Percy Lovell's family. You remember them, Sue—" he turned to his sister "—three children—two boys, one girl— all under the age of five."

Lady Susan repressed a shudder and replied that she could not possibly forget the Lovells, particularly the children, who were abominable brats not above sneaking frogs into their mother's parlour while she was entertaining her friends.

"Yes, but they have graduated from frogs to snakes, or so Percy tells me. And they are only abominable because they don't have the proper governess."

"But why are you talking about governesses?" Lady Aldyth exclaimed.

"Because Davida wishes to become one," Lyall said.

Lady Aldyth turned stricken eyes to her daughter. "Oh, Davida, no! You must be jesting. Not that governesses are so horrid, for I must say the ones we had for you and Cassie were always so congenial, but really, that's hardly the future I want for you!"

At this point the Reverend Bell, who had been listening to a conversation of no interest except to widowers or governesses, demanded to know which couple he was to marry that day.

Lady Aldyth, reminded of the presence of the minister, put one hand on the marquis's arm.

"Alwyn and I. Cassie and her captain, and," she said, swallowing hard, "Davida and her Jeremy."

Davida's eyes flashed with anger. "You and Cassie may marry whomever you wish, Mama," she said scorchingly.

"But I am not about to be forced into marriage with Lyall. And as for calling him 'my Jeremy,' words fail me."

"Yes," Lady Susan murmured sympathetically. "So true. Lyall can be so odious and at times a slow top, particularly when it comes to romance. But on the other hand, do you really think you will dislike marrying him that much? I confess I have got quite used to thinking of you as a sister. And since meeting you, Lyall himself has seemed a shade less dissolute."

"Thank you, Susan," her brother answered. "I accept all such homage with appropriate blushes." Nevertheless he made a determined move past his sister and toward the door.

"Jeremy!" She caught his arm. "You are not leaving!"

"No," he replied, his eyes glinting. "But you are. All of you."

"Leaving?" Lady Susan looked shocked.

"Yes, if you don't mind fulfilling the request of a slow top?"

"Oh, I see! Leaving!" Lady Susan smiled in perfect understanding. "Yes, I do think that's a good idea. We should all leave now. I knew it would take time," she whispered to Lady Aldyth and Cassie, "but I do believe he is starting to see the light. Come along, Captain," she said, detaching that gentleman from his claret. "No, not you, Davida. You sit there on the couch. I just know that my brother has something quite intriguing to say to you."

Lyall closed the door with a grimace. Feeling uncharacteristically nervous, Davida discovered that she was sitting upon the couch that Lady Susan had designated, and she rose instantly, preferring to meet any challenge from a standing position.

"I don't wish to hear a word from you," she warned as he moved towards her.

"What a pity. I had a particularly good speech all prepared. One I'm sure even Mr. Edmund Kean would have approved of."

"Don't think you can force me—"

Lyall looked disappointed. "Come, come, Miss Cooper. It is too late in the day to indulge in melodrama, which is so fatiguing, don't you agree? I have no intention of forcing you, as you put it, to marry me."

"Well, good," she said, conscious of another conflicting emotion within. "For my marrying you has to be the most idiotish idea I've ever heard."

He nodded his agreement. "I thought so myself the first time I heard of it, from you."

"From me?" she cried out, then subsided. "You are talking about that odious contract, are you not?"

"Of course I am talking about that odious contract," Lyall retorted. "Everything revolves around that contract, including my future, which may not hold much fascination for you but is of rather absorbing interest to me. And I need to know if you plan to enforce it."

"Enforce the contract?" She looked up into his handsome face.

He nodded. "You could. There I'd be, tied hand and foot to the altar at St. George's, Hanover Square, just waiting for you to march down the aisle and snatch me up."

Davida, while acknowledging that the idea of Lyall tied hand and foot to an altar certainly was a spectacle of merit, pronounced her unwillingness to bear the burden of the amusement.

"I have no intention of snatching you up."

Lyall let out a sigh of relief. "Good. I should hate to have that hanging over my head like an axe," he said, looking so cheerful that she felt a tiny pang of resentment—no doubt the product of a long and arduous day.

"I don't see why you're so interested in the contract."

"I'd be delighted to tell you, but first—" he pointed to the couch "—my legs are rather tired."

Davida sat down on the couch, smoothing the folds of her dress.

"Now, first I must hear it from your lips, that you are withdrawing from the contract."

"Oh, very well," she said, wondering if that was all he had on his wretched mind. "I am withdrawing my claim under the contract. Are you satisfied?"

"Yes, I believe I am," he answered with a happy smile.

Blinking hard, Davida rose from the couch. "Now that that is settled I should like to join the others," she said.

But a firm hand immediately locked on her wrist. "Not yet, my dear," Lyall said softly.

"Lord Lyall, I must insist."

"And I must insist," he told her, drawing her down on the couch again. "I must insist that you listen to my offer of marriage before quitting this room."

For a brief moment the world swam before Davida's eyes. "Offer of marriage?" she repeated, noticing that his eyes were smiling down at her. "But you have just finished insisting that I withdraw."

Lyall grinned. "I don't relish being coerced into anything, especially marriage, any more than you, my dear. And what gentleman could really propose properly to a lady who has the right to hold him to a stupid contract their fathers drew up one night when they were foxed?"

"Lyall, are you proposing to me?" Davida asked, dazed and feeling as though she were in a dream, one she wished never to be wakened from.

"Yes," he said with a laugh. "And I know full well I am making a mull of it. All the pretty words I had prepared have scattered to the wind. Believe it or not—" he smiled ruefully down at her "—this is the first occasion I've had to offer for anyone, in spite of the fact that ten minutes ago I was engaged to your charming sister.'' He pressed her hand to his lips.

"But really, Lyall, you can't mean you want to marry me. It's just Mama's ridiculous notion of three weddings to be performed."

Lyall was laughing in earnest. "Davida, Davida, if I had no humility before meeting you, I assure you I have earned a full portion of it now."

"But we can't marry. I vow we don't even like each other as a rule."

"Rules, Miss Cooper, were made to be broken," he answered, cupping her chin firmly in his hand. "For myself I confess that the mere notion of living without you by my side to vex and scold me is enough to sink me into the depths of despair. Susan's little scheme worked better than she realized. When I thought you had absconded with the captain I saw red. You can ask Cassie."

Davida's eyes searched his. "Are you saying you love me?"

"Of course, I love you. Look into my eyes," he commanded. "See how they yearn?" A giggle burst unbidden from them both. "Furthermore," he ordered, "you must marry me quickly, for I cannot stand the mortifying possibility of being jilted by another member of the same family. Unlike Hugh, I have no Miss Baugh waiting in the wings."

"But you are not Hugh," Davida said thankfully as he lowered his lips to hers in the manner he had recommended minutes ago to the captain and Cassie.

Davida returned his embrace, her heart pumping wildly and her senses nearing intoxication. The kiss erased whatever doubts had lingered in her mind.

"Well," Lyall demanded, sounding a little shaky.

"Well, what?" she asked demurely, playing with a button on his coat.

"Do you love me, minx?"

She laughed. "What do my eyes say?"

He held her off. "They say to kiss you again," he answered, and promptly did so. "You'll marry me," he said as she snuggled back into his arms.

"You're hounding me—" she sighed "—just as I always knew you would."

Five minutes later the parlour door opened a crack, and Lyall, frowning, watched his sister step gingerly forward.

"I know I shouldn't bother you at such a time, Jeremy," she said apologetically. "But it is that dreadful minister, Reverend Bell. Really the most impatient of creatures, which I consider a serious flaw in a man of his calling. He insists on knowing how many ceremonies he is to perform today. One, two, or . . . ?" She paused delicately.

"Well, Miss Cooper?" Lyall asked, gazing down at Davida with eyes which, no doubt about it, did yearn.

Davida, tucked happily in the crook of his arm, smiled up at him. "Three has always been rumoured to be lucky," she acknowledged.

"So it has," Lady Susan said, much struck by this wisdom. Beaming benevolently at them both, she went off to inform the impatient Reverend Bell that three weddings would constitute his afternoon's work.

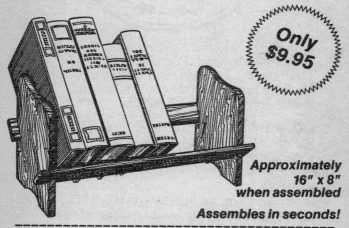

PAMELA BROWNING

... is fireworks on the green at the Fourth of July and prayers said around the Thanksgiving table. It is the dream of freedom realized in thousands of small towns across this great nation.

But mostly, the Heartland is its people. People who care about and help one another. People who cherish traditional values and give to their children the greatest gift, the gift of love.

American Romance presents HEARTLAND, an emotional trilogy about people whose memories, hopes and dreams are bound up in the acres they farm.

HEARTLAND ... the story of America.

Don't miss these heartfelt stories: American Romance #237 SIMPLE GIFTS (March), #241 FLY AWAY (April), and #245 HARVEST HOME (May).

HRT-1

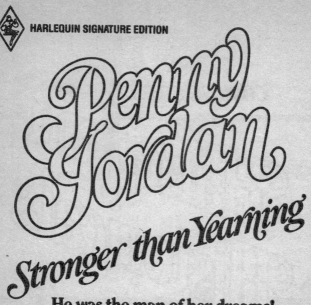

Penny Jordan

Stronger than Yearning

He was the man of her dreams!

The same dark hair, the same mocking eyes; it was as if the Regency rake of the portrait, the seducer of Jenna's dream, had come to life. Jenna, believing the last of the Deverils dead, was determined to buy the great old Yorkshire Hall—to claim it for her daughter, Lucy, and put to rest some of the painful memories of Lucy's birth. She had no way of knowing that a direct descendant of the black sheep Deveril even existed—or that James Allingham and his own powerful yearnings would disrupt her plan entirely.

Penny Jordan's first Harlequin Signature Edition *Love's Choices* was an outstanding success. Penny Jordan has written more than 40 best-selling titles—more than 4 million copies sold.

Now, be sure to buy her latest bestseller, *Stronger Than Yearning*. Available wherever paperbacks are sold—in June.